ROUGH RIDER

New York Times Bestselling Author

B.J. DANIELS

HARLEQUIN INTRIGUE®

This book is for Anita Green, who opened a quilt shop in our little town. There is nothing like sitting in her shop after a long day writing and dreaming of new projects—both writing and quilting.

ISBN-13: 978-1-335-72125-9

Recycling programs for this product may not exist in your area.

Rough Rider

Copyright © 2017 by Barbara Heinlein

Printed in U.S.A.

B.J. Daniels is a *New York Times* and *USA TODAY* bestselling author. She wrote her first book after a career as an award-winning newspaper journalist and author of thirty-seven published short stories. She lives in Montana with her husband, Parker, and three springer spaniels. When not writing, she quilts, boats and plays tennis. Contact her at bjdaniels.com, on Facebook or on Twitter, @bjdanielsauthor.

Books by B.J. Daniels

Harlequin Intrigue

Whitehorse, Montana: The McGraw Kidnapping

Dark Horse
Rough Rider

Whitehorse, Montana

Secret of Deadman's Coulee
The New Deputy in Town
The Mystery Man of Whitehorse
Classified Christmas
Matchmaking with a Mission
Second Chance Cowboy
Montana Royalty
Shotgun Bride

Visit the Author Profile page at Harlequin.com.

CAST OF CHARACTERS

Boone McGraw—The cowboy went to Butte, Montana, hoping to find his sister who'd been kidnapped twenty-five years ago. Instead, he found more than he bargained for.

C.J. Knight—The private investigator didn't have time for the handsome cowboy from Whitehorse. She had to find her PI partner's killer.

Jesse Rose McGraw—She'd been taken from her crib when she was six months old. If she was still alive twenty-five years later, her family was determined to find her.

Hank Knight—The private investigator had kept a lot of secrets from his young female partner. But were they secrets that had gotten him killed?

Jim Waters—The McGraw family attorney was suspect, but what was he really guilty of?

Blake Ryan—The former McGraw ranch manager had managed to stay out of the line of fire for a while at least. But now he, too, was being investigated.

Matilda "Tilly" Marks—The ranch housekeeper had always loved listening in on what was going on at the ranch. But this time, she might have shared it with the wrong person.

Cecil Marks—He would do anything to keep his wife, Tilly, and stay out of trouble. But trouble had never been far behind him.

Patricia McGraw—The second wife of Travers McGraw and former nanny was ready to tell everything from her jail cell.

Chapter One

Boone McGraw parked the pickup at the edge of the dark, deserted city street and checked the address again. One look around at the boarded-up old buildings in Butte's uptown and he feared his suspicions had been warranted.

Christmas lights glowed in the valley below. But uptown on what had once been known as the richest hill on earth, there was no sign of the approaching holiday. Shoving back his Stetson, he let out a long sigh. He feared the information the family attorney had allegedly received was either wrong or an attempted con job. It wouldn't be the first time someone had tried to cash in on the family's tragedy.

But he'd promised his father, Travers McGraw, that he would follow up on the lead. Not that he believed for a moment that it was going to help him find Jesse Rose, his sister, who'd been kidnapped from her crib twenty-five years ago.

Boone glanced toward the dilapidated building

that reportedly housed Knight Investigations. According to the family's former lawyer, Jim Waters, he'd spoken to a private investigator by the name of Hank Knight a few times on the phone. Knight had asked questions that supposedly had Waters suspecting that the PI knew something more than he was saying. But Waters had never met with the man. All he'd had for Boone to go on was a phone number and an address.

The phone had recently been disconnected and the century-old brick building looked completely abandoned with dusty for-lease signs in most of the windows and just dust in others. No lights burned in the building—not that he'd expected anyone to be working this late.

Boone told himself that he might as well get a motel for the night and come back tomorrow. Not that he expected to find anything here. He was convinced this long trip from Whitehorse to Butte had been a wild-goose chase.

His father had been easy prey for twenty-five years. Desperate to find the missing twins who'd been kidnapped, Travers had appealed to every news outlet. Anyone who'd watched the news or picked up a newspaper over the past twenty-five years knew how desperate he was since each year, the amount of the reward for information had grown.

Boone, suspicious by nature, had been skeptical

from the get-go. The family attorney had proven he couldn't be trusted. So why trust information he said he'd gotten? His father hadn't trusted the lawyer for some time—with good reason. He swore under his breath. All he could think about was how disappointed his father was going to be—and not for the first time.

But he'd promised he would track down the PI and follow up on the information no matter what it took. And damn if he wouldn't, he thought as he started his pickup. But before he could pull away, he caught movement out of the corner of his eye. A dark figure had just come around the block and was now moving quickly down the sidewalk. The figure slowed at the building that housed Knight Investigations. He watched as the person slipped in through the only door at the front.

Across the street, Boone shut off the truck's engine and waited. He told himself the person he'd seen could be homeless and merely looking for a place to sleep. It was late and the fall night was clear and cold at this high altitude. Butte sat at 5,538 feet above sea level and often had snow on the ground a good portion of the year.

Boone hunkered in the dark, watching the building until he began to lose patience with himself. This was a waste of his time. The cab of the truck was getting cold. What he needed was a warm bed. A warm meal didn't sound bad, either. He could come back in the morning and—

A light flickered on behind one of the windows on the top floor and began to bob around the room. Someone was up there with a flashlight. He squinted, able to finally make out the lettering on the warbled old glass: Knight Investigations.

He felt his pulse thrum under his skin. It appeared he wasn't the only one interested in Hank Knight.

Chapter Two

Climbing out and locking the rig, Boone headed for the door where he'd seen the figure disappear inside. A sliver of moon hung over the mountains that ringed Butte. Stars twinkled like ice crystals in the midnight blue sky overhead. Boone could see his breath as he crossed the street.

The moment he opened the door, he was hit with the musky scent of the old building. He stopped just inside to listen, but heard nothing. Seeing the out-of-order sign on the ancient elevator, he turned to the door marked Stairs, opened it and saw that a naked bulb dangled from the ceiling giving off dim light. He began to climb, taking three steps at a time.

As he neared the top floor, he slowed and quieted the sound of his boot soles as best he could on the wooden stairs. Pushing open the door marked Fifth Floor, he listened for a moment, then stepped out. A single bulb glowed faintly overhead, another halfway down the long empty hallway.

The building was eerily quiet. No lights shone under any of the doors to his right. To his left, toward the front of the building, he saw that there were four doors.

The last door, where he estimated Knight Investigations should be, was ajar. A faint light glowed from within.

As quietly as possible, he moved down the hall, telling himself maybe Hank had come back for something. Or someone else was looking for something in the detective's office.

He was almost to the doorway when he stopped to listen. Someone was in there banging around, opening and closing metal file cabinet drawers. Definitely searching for something.

Boone leaned around the edge of the doorjamb to look into the office. In the ambient light of the intruder's flashlight, he saw nothing but an old large oak desk, a worn leather chair behind it and a couple of equally worn chairs in front of it. Along the wall were a half dozen file cabinets, most of them open. There seemed to be files strewn everywhere.

With Knight Investigations' phone disconnected, he had assumed Hank had closed down the business. Possibly taken off in a hurry. Now, seeing that the man had even left behind his office furniture as well as file cabinets full of cases, that seemed like a viable explanation. Hank Knight was on the lam.

His pulse jumped at the thought. Was it possible he did know something about Jesse Rose and the kidnapping? Is that why he'd taken off like he apparently had?

Boone couldn't see the intruder—only the flashlight beam low on the other side of the desk. He could hear movement. It sounded as if the intruder was rustling through papers on the floor behind the desk. Looking for something in particular? Or a homeless person just piling up papers to make a fire in the chilly office?

Stepping closer, Boone slowly pushed the door open a little wider. The door creaked. The intruder didn't seem to hear it, but he froze for a moment anyway. For all he knew, the person going through papers on the floor behind the desk could be armed and dangerous—if not crazy and drugged up.

Pushing the door all the way open, he carefully stepped in. He took in the crowded office in the ambient light of the intruder's flashlight beam. The office had clearly been ransacked. Files were all over the floor and desk.

He realized that this intruder hadn't had enough time to make this much of a mess. Someone had already been here. Which meant this new intruder was probably too late for whatever he was searching for. If that's what he was doing hidden on the other side of the desk.

The line of old metal file cabinets along the wall all had their drawers hanging open. In the middle of all this mess, the large old oak desk was almost indistinguishable because of piles of papers, dirty coffee cups and stacks of files.

He moved closer, still unable to see the intruder, who appeared to be busy on the floor behind the large worn leather office chair on the other side of the cluttered desk.

The flashlight beam suddenly stilled. Had the intruder heard him?

Boone reached into his pocket, found his cell phone, but stopped short of calling 911. His family had been in the news for years. If the cops came, so would the media. He swore under his breath and withdrew his hand sans the cell phone.

Boone had a bad feeling that anchored itself in the pit of his stomach. He reminded himself that the person behind that desk might be someone more dangerous than he was in the mood to take on tonight.

He looked around for something he could use as a weapon. He had no desire to play hero. He'd always been smart enough to pick and choose his battles. This wasn't one he wanted to lose for a wild-goose chase. Seeing nothing worthy of being a weapon, he took a step back.

The person on the other side of the desk had

stopped making a sound. The beam of the flashlight hadn't moved for a full minute.

He took another step back. The floorboards groaned under his weight. He swore under his breath as suddenly the flashlight beam swooped across the ceiling. The figure shot up from behind the office chair. All he caught was a flash of wild copper-colored hair—and the dull shine of a handgun—before the light blinded him.

Instinctively, he took another step backward. One more and he could dive out into the hallway—

"Take another step and you're a dead man."

He froze at the sound of a woman's voice—and the imminent threat in it. Not to mention the laser dot that had appeared over his heart.

C.J. STARED AT the cowboy standing just inside the door. The gun in her hand never wavered. Nor did the red laser dot pointed at his heart move a fraction of an inch. He was a big man, broad-shouldered, slim-hipped and rugged-looking. He wore Western attire, including a Stetson as if straight off the ranch.

"Easy," he said, his voice deep and soft, but nonetheless threatening. "I'm just here looking for Hank Knight."

"Why?"

He frowned, holding up one hand to shield his eyes from the flashlight she also had on him. "That's between him and me. How about I call the cops so they can ask you why you're ransacking his office." He started to reach into his pocket.

She lowered the flashlight so she was no longer blinding him and shook her head. "I wouldn't do that if I were you," she said, motioning with the gun. "Who are you and why do you want to see Hank?"

"Why should I tell *you*?" She could see that he was taking her measure. He could overpower her easily enough given his size—and hers. But then again, there was that "equalizer" in her hand.

"You should tell me because I have a gun pointed at your heart—and I'm Hank's partner. C.J. West."

He seemed to chew on that for a moment before he said, "Boone McGraw."

She took in the name. "Kidnapping case," she said, more to herself than to him. Fraternal twins, six months old, taken from their cribs over twenty-five years ago. A ransom was paid but the twins were never returned. That was the extent of what she knew and even that was vague. The only reason she knew this was because of something she'd recently seen on television. There'd been an update. One of the kidnappers had been found dead.

"Your partner was looking into the case."

"That's not possible."

"Our lawyer spoke with him on two different occasions, so I'm afraid it definitely happened. So how about lowering the gun?"

Frowning, she considered what he'd said, still skeptical. She and Hank talked about all their cases. It wouldn't have been like him to keep a possible case like this from her.

But she did lower the gun, tucking it into the waistband of her jeans—just in case.

"Thanks. Now, if you could please tell me where I can find him…"

"Day after tomorrow he will be in Rosemont Cemetery."

He'd been looking around the office, but now his gaze shot back to her. *"Cemetery?"*

"He was killed by a hit-and-run driver three days ago." Her voice cracked. It still didn't seem real, but it always came with a wave of grief and pain.

"A *hit-and-run*?"

She wondered if he planned to keep echoing everything she said. She really didn't have time for this.

"Clearly you're too late. Not that Hank could have known anything about the kidnapping case." Picking up one of Hank's files, she shone the flashlight on it and then began to thumb through the yellow notebook pages inside.

Not that she didn't watch Boone McGraw—if that was really his name—out of the corner of her eye.

She'd learned never to take anything at face value. Hank had taught her that and a lot more.

The cowboy swore as he looked around the destroyed office. His expression said he wasn't ready to give up. "If you're his partner then why is the Knight Investigations phone disconnected and this office without electricity?"

"Hank was in the process of retiring. I have my own office in my home. I was taking over the business."

"So you hadn't spoken for a while?" He was guessing, but he'd guessed right.

"We were in transition."

"So you can't be sure he didn't know something about the kidnapping case."

She gritted her teeth. This cowboy was impossible. "Hank would have told me if he knew something about the case. I'm sorry you've wasted your time." She just wanted him to leave so she could get back to what she was doing.

Since Hank's so-called accident, she'd been hard-pressed to hold it together. All that kept her going was her anger and determination to find his killer. She was convinced that one of his cases had gotten him murdered. All she had to do was figure out which one.

The cowboy moved, but only to step deeper into

the room. "You said he was killed three days ago? Is that when he returned from his trip?"

"His trip?" Now she was starting to sound like him.

He frowned and jammed his hands on his hips as he looked at her. "My father's lawyer talked to him over two weeks ago. Your partner told him that he was going to be away and would get back to us. When we didn't hear from him…"

She shook her head. "He didn't go anywhere."

"Then why did he lie to our lawyer? Unless he had something to hide?"

C.J. threw down the files in her hands with impatience. "Mr. McGraw—"

"Boone."

"Boone, you didn't know Hank, but I did. He wouldn't have lied."

"Then how do you explain what he told our lawyer?"

She couldn't and that bothered her. She studied the cowboy for a minute. Had Hank gone on a trip— just as he'd told the McGraw lawyer? C.J. thought of how distracted Hank had been the last time she'd seen him. He hadn't mentioned talking to anyone connected to the McGraw kidnapping and for a man who loved to talk about his cases, that was more than unusual.

A case like that didn't come along every day, especially given Knight Investigations' clients. But it also wasn't the kind of case Hank would be interested in. If it was true and he'd called the McGraw lawyer, he must have merely out of curiosity.

She said as much and picked up more files.

"It wasn't idle curiosity." Boone stepped closer until only the large cluttered desk stood between them. He loomed over it. His presence alone could have sucked all the air out of the room. Fortunately, all he did was make her too aware of just how male he was. He didn't intimidate her, not even for a moment. At least that's what she told herself.

"I guess we'll never know, will we?" she said, meeting his steely gaze with one of her hard blue ones.

"If there is even a chance that he knew the whereabouts of my sister, Jesse Rose, then I'm not leaving town until I find out the truth. Starting with whether or not Hank Knight recently left town. It should be easy enough to find out. How much?"

C.J. stared at him. "How much what?"

"How much *money*? I want to hire you."

Chapter Three

Boone was surprised by the young woman's reaction.

"Sorry, but I'm not available." She actually sounded offended.

"Because you're too busy going through dusty old files?"

She looked up from where she was leafing through one and slowly put it down. "The reason my partner is dead is in one of these files. I need to find his killer."

"Wait, I thought it was an accident?"

"That's what the police say, but they're wrong."

He shook his head. He'd run into his share of stubborn women, but this one took the cake. "You seem pretty sure of yourself about a lot of things."

She put her hands on her hips and looked like she could chew nails. "Hank was murdered. I'd stake my life on it."

"If you're right, then there is probably a good chance that's what you're doing."

"He would have done the same for me. Hank…
Everyone loved him."

Well, not everyone, but he knew now wasn't the
time to point that out. He could see how hard this
was on her and told himself to cut her some slack.
But if he had any hope of finding out if Hank Knight
had known where his kidnapped sister was, then he
needed this woman's help.

"I'm sorry. Apparently the two of you were close,"
he said, which surprised him since Waters had said
Hank Knight was elderly. She'd just said the man
was in the process of retiring.

Hank's advancing age could be the reason he had
such a young partner. In the ambient glow of the
flashlight C.J. didn't even look thirty, though given
her confidence, she could have been older. Her long
curly hair was the deep, rich color of copper, framing
a face flecked with freckles. Both made her brown
eyes look wider and more innocent. She had her un-
ruly hair pulled back into a ponytail and wore an
old Cubs baseball cap. His father had always been a
huge Cubs fan. Boone wondered if Hank had been.

C.J. West was a slight woman but one he knew
better than to underestimate. He needed her help because the more he thought about it, the more he felt
the answers were here in Butte, here in this office.

"I've known Hank since I was a child playing in
this building," she said. "My mother had a job on an-

other floor. I used to hang out with him. He taught me everything I know about the investigative business plus much more. He was like a father to me."

Boone nodded. "I can't imagine how hard this is for you. I hate that I have to add to your problems at a time like this, but let's say you're right and your partner was murdered. Why an old case? Why not the McGraw kidnapping? One of the kidnappers is still at large. If your partner knew something and made inquiries that alerted the kidnapper..."

He was winging it, but he saw that at least she was considering it. Of course, there was also the chance that Hank Knight's death was just an accident. That the man had merely been curious about the McGraw kidnapping case. That all of this was a waste of time.

But Boone had always gone on instinct and right now his instincts told him he had to get this woman to help him. If Hank had been telling the truth and he'd left town, then maybe where he'd gone would lead them to Jesse Rose—and her partner's killer.

ACROSS THE STREET from the Knight Investigations office, Cecil Marks slumped down in his vehicle to watch the office of Knight Investigations. He'd been worried when he'd heard that there might be a break in the kidnapping case. That some private investigator in Butte might know not just where Jesse Rose was, but might also know who was the second kidnapper—

the one who'd handed the babies out the window to the man on the ladder.

After twenty-five years, he'd thought for sure that the truth would never come out. Now he wasn't so sure. He'd known that Boone McGraw was like a dog with a bone when it came to not letting go of something. The moment he'd heard about Hank Knight and Knight Investigations, he'd known he had to take care of it.

Once he came to Butte and found out that Hank Knight was retiring, he'd told himself that no one would tie the kidnapping to the old PI.

But unfortunately, he hadn't known about the man's partner. It was her up there now with Boone McGraw. He doubted they would find anything. He hadn't when he'd searched the office, and he'd been thorough. He'd left the place in such a mess, even if he had missed something, he doubted it would turn up now.

It was cold in his truck without the motor running, but he didn't want to call attention to himself. As badly as he wanted to go back to the motel where he was staying, he had to be sure they didn't find anything. Once Boone went back to Whitehorse, he figured he wouldn't have to worry anymore.

He told himself that the little gal partner, C.J. West, wouldn't be searching the office if she knew anything. Also if she knew, he would have heard by now.

She suspected the hit-and-run hadn't been an accident. But there was no proof. Nor did he think the cops were even looking all that hard. He'd seen something on the news and only a footnote in the newspaper. Hank Knight had been a two-bit PI nobody. Look at that heap of an office he worked out of.

He tried to reassure himself that he was in the clear. That nothing would come of any of this. He'd done what he'd had to do and he would do it again. His hands began to shake at the thought, though, of being forced to kill yet another person, especially a woman.

But if she and Boone didn't stop, he'd have no choice.

C.J. HATED TO admit that the cowboy might be right. Before Boone McGraw had walked into this office, she'd been sure Hank's death had something to do with one of his older cases. All of his newer cases that he'd told her about were nothing that could get a man killed—at least she didn't think so.

Now she had to adjust her thinking. Could this be about the kidnapping? Her mind balked because Hank loved nothing better than to talk about his cases. He wouldn't have been able *not* to talk about this one unless… Unless he did know something, something that he thought could put her in danger…

"Why do you think the hit-and-run wasn't an accident?" the cowboy asked.

It took her a moment to get her thoughts together. "This ransacked office for one. Clearly someone was looking for something in the old files."

"You're that sure it involved a case?"

She waved a hand through the air. "Why tear up the office unless the killer is looking for the case file—and whatever incriminating evidence might be in it?"

He nodded as if that made sense to him. "But if it was here, don't you think that whoever did this took the file with him?"

"Actually, I don't. Look at this place. I'd say the person got frustrated when he didn't find it. Otherwise, why trash the place?"

"You have a point. But let's say the file you're looking for is about the McGraw kidnapping. It wouldn't be an old file since he called only a few weeks ago. When did he turn off his phone and electricity here at the office?"

C.J. hated to admit that she didn't know. "We've both been busy on separate cases. But he would have told me if he knew anything about the case." He wouldn't have kept something like that from her, she kept telling herself. And yet he hadn't mentioned talking to the McGraw lawyer and her instincts told her that Boone McGraw wasn't lying about that.

That Hank now wouldn't have the opportunity to tell her hit her hard. Hank had been like family, her only family, and now he was gone. And she was only starting to realize how much Hank had been keeping from her.

She had to look away, not wanting Boone to see the shine of tears that burned her eyes. She wouldn't break down. Especially in front of this cowboy.

"If Hank did know something about the case, would he have started a file?" the cowboy asked as he picked up a stack of files from the floor, straightened them and then stacked them on the edge of the desk.

"He would have written something down, I suppose."

"But wouldn't have started a file."

C.J. sighed. "No, but you're assuming a twenty-five-year-old kidnapping is what got him killed. It wasn't the kind of case he worked. Not to mention that Butte is miles from Whitehorse, Montana. The chances that Hank knew anything about the kidnapping or the whereabouts of your sister, Jesse Rose—"

"Are slim. I agree. But I can't discount it. He called our attorney. He knew something or he wouldn't have done that. I don't think he was curious and I don't think you do, either."

She wanted to argue. The cowboy brought that

out in her. But she couldn't. "Fine, let's say he did know something."

"So where are his notes?"

C.J. shot him a disbelieving glance as she raised her hands to take in the ransacked room. "Let me just grab them for you."

"I'd be happy to help you look."

"I don't need your help," she said. "For all I know, you're the one who tore the place apart."

"And then came back to confront you and pretend to look for my own file? How clever of me. If I couldn't find it when this place wasn't a mess, why would I think you could now?"

She saw the logic, but hated to admit it. "Or maybe you didn't find what you were looking for and hope that I'll find it for you."

He grinned. "I admire the way your mind works, though I find it a little disturbing."

C.J. bristled. Was he flirting with her?

"You really think I'm the killer cozying up to the partner? Pretty darned gutsy of me." He shook his head. "Hit-and-run is a coward's way of killing. Your killer wouldn't have the guts to come waltzing in here and face you." He had a point. "But don't you want to call the cops and report the break-in before you destroy any more evidence?"

"I ALREADY CALLED THEM."

Boone heard the anger in her voice as he noticed

the old photographs framed on the walls. "They weren't helpful?" he asked as he got up to inspect them with the flashlight on his cell phone. The snapshots were of the same man, Hank Knight, no doubt, with a variety of prominent men and women and even a couple of celebrities. From the looks of the photos they were old. Which meant Hank Knight had been doing this for years.

"The local cops, helpful?" C.J. let out a laugh. "They don't believe the hit-and-run was murder because we normally don't take those kinds of cases."

"I would think any kind of case could turn violent under the wrong circumstances," he said, turning from the photographs on the wall. "Look, I'm not leaving town until I get some answers. So what do you say? Let me at least help you look through the files. Other than one on the McGraw kidnapping, what are we looking for?"

She glanced up at him and her gaze softened a little toward him as he took off his coat and rolled up the sleeves of his Western shirt. "Fine. While you're looking for something on the kidnapping, keep an eye out for any recent entries, even in the old files." She showed him what to look for on one of the files. "Hank had his own way of doing things."

"I can see that," Boone said as he scooped up more folders.

"We did work closely. Until recently. I did a lot of

the legwork. I have to admit, the last few weeks… I hadn't seen much of Hank."

So, just as he'd guessed, she was looking for a needle in a haystack and had no idea what had gotten her partner killed. He dropped the folders on the desk next to the others and began going through them quickly. "I suppose you know from the news. One of the kidnappers was found. Dead, unfortunately, so one is still out there. But it's put the kidnapping back in the news. More information was released. That's why I assume your partner called. Also my brother Oakley's been found, although that information hasn't been released."

She looked up in obvious surprise. "I thought the man who came forward proved to be a fraud?"

Boone nodded. "Vance Elliot was an impostor, but surprisingly he helped flush out my real biological brother. The news media doesn't know about it because he doesn't want the publicity, which I can't blame him for. In fact, he wants nothing to do with my family. Another reason why I need to find Jesse Rose. Hopefully, *she* won't break our father's heart."

THE NEWS TOOK C.J. by surprise. A son who wanted nothing to do with his family? The subject, though, appeared to be closed as he went back to work. Not that she wasn't curious, but right now she had to find out who had wanted Hank dead.

Sometimes she forgot he was gone. She'd spent so many hours in this office with him growing up... She swallowed the sudden lump in her throat. Hank had meant everything to her. The thought of him being gone... She pushed it away, telling herself she owed it to him to find his killer. That's what she had to focus on right now. Later she would have time for grief, for regrets, for the pain that lay just beneath the surface.

She reached for more files from the floor, her fingers trembling. She stopped to squeeze her hands into fists for a moment. If there was one thing C.J. hated to show, it was any kind of weakness. Maybe especially to a man like Boone McGraw. She could look at the set of his jaw or gaze into those frosty blue eyes and she knew what kind of man he was. Stubbornly strong, like a tree that had lived through everything thrown at it for all its years. Just like Hank.

"It's not here," Boone said after an hour had passed. "Unless your partner didn't write it down. Or if he did, whoever tore up this place took the information with him."

With a sigh, C.J. carried a handful of case files over to one of the cabinets and set them inside just to get them out of the way. Files were everywhere. Then again, this was pretty normal for Hank's office. He'd never been organized. It was one reason they'd never been able to share an office.

She took a moment before she turned to look at Boone McGraw. The cowboy took up a lot of space. The broad shoulders, the towering height—all that maleness culminated into one handsome, cocky cowboy. She bet most women swooned at his feet and was glad she wasn't one of them.

"So we're back to square one," she said, sounding as discouraged as she felt. She'd looked through all of the files, including those that Boone had also looked through. Not only hadn't she found anything about the McGraw kidnapping, she hadn't seen any old case that might have gotten Hank killed.

"Not necessarily," Boone said as he put both palms on the desk and leaned toward her. "Your partner knew something about the kidnapping. Hank Knight asked questions about Jesse Rose and an item that was taken from her crib the night she was kidnapped. His questions led our lawyer to believe Hank had knowledge about the crime and possibly where Jesse Rose is now. I think he got too close to the truth. Too close to the kidnapper's accomplice. And if I'm right then you can help me prove it."

Chapter Four

C.J. pulled up Hank's old leather chair and dropped into it. She was too tired, too wrung out, too filled with grief to take on this cowboy. Nor could she see how she would be able to prove anything.

She pushed a stack of old files out of the way and dropped her elbows to the top of the scarred desk to rest her chin in her hands. She watched Boone McGraw pick up files and put them back into the filing cabinets. He was actually cleaning up the office. The sight would have made her laugh, if she'd had the energy.

What she needed was sleep. She hadn't had a good night's sleep since Hank's death. She doubted she would tonight, but sitting here wasn't helping. As she started to get up, she pushed off the desk only to have the worn top shift under her hands.

With a start she remembered something she'd seen Hank do when he was interrupted by a walk-in. Sitting back, she felt into the crack between the old oak desktop and the even older one beneath it. Hank had loved this desk and hadn't been able to part with it even after one of his cigars had burned the original top badly. Rather than replace it, he'd simply covered it up.

She'd seen files disappear from view only to be retrieved later after a client left. Her fingers brushed against something that felt like the edge of a file folder. She worked it out, her heart leaping up into her throat as she saw the name printed on it in Hank's neat script: McGraw.

"Did you find something?" Boone asked, stopping his organizing to step closer.

She looked up, having forgotten about him for a moment. When had Hank shoved this file into the crack? Who would have walked in that he didn't want them to see it? Her heart began to pound. Until that moment, she had refused to believe that Hank would have taken the McGraw kidnapping case— let alone that it could have anything to do with getting him killed.

C.J. tried to remember the last time she'd stopped by Hank's office. The thousands of times all melted together. Had he ever furtively hidden a file when *she'd* walked in? Had he the last time she saw him alive, just hours before he was struck down and killed?

Her fingers were trembling as she opened the file

and saw that there was only one sheet of yellow lined notebook paper—the kind Hank always used. There were also only a few words written on it, several phone numbers and some doodling off to one side. She read the words: "Travers McGraw, Sundown Stallion Station, Whitehorse, Montana. Oakley, Jesse Rose, six months old. Stuffed toy horse. Pink ribbon. Pink grosgrain ribbon."

BOONE HAD SEEN her expression when she'd pulled the manila file folder out from what appeared to be a crack between the new desktop and the old warped one. She'd found something that had made her pale.

"May I?" he asked again.

Silently, C.J. handed over the file, crossed her arms and watched as Boone opened it as if she'd known he was going to be disappointed.

"Where's the rest of it?" he said after looking at the words written on the yellow-lined sheet of paper inside.

"That's all there is."

He could see that she was shaken by what she'd found. Not only had Hank started a file, he'd hidden it. That had to mean something given how the color had drained from her face and how shaken she still looked.

She started around the desk, bumped into him as she stumbled into an unstable stack of files. He caught her, his hands going around her slim waist as she clutched at him for a moment before she got her balance and pulled free. She headed toward a small door he hadn't noticed before. As she opened it, he saw it was a compact bathroom.

Boone turned his attention back to the file as she closed the door. So Hank Knight *had* started a file. But if he'd found out anything, there was no indication of it. Maybe the man didn't know anything about Jesse Rose. Maybe he *was* just curious.

Or maybe not, he realized as he stared at the notes the PI had taken. He'd known about the stuffed toy horse. But he'd also known about the pink ribbon around its neck—something that hadn't been released to the press.

He studied the doodling on the side of the page. Hank had drawn a little girl with chin-length hair. His depiction of Jesse Rose from his imagination? Or his memory? Beside the girl, Hank had drawn what looked like a little dog.

A few moments later, he heard the toilet flush. C.J. came out drying her hands on a paper towel. He studied her for a moment. She seemed different somehow. She looked stronger, more assured. He realized she'd probably used the bathroom to get over the shock of finding the hidden file. But what about it had shaken her? The realization that he could be right?

"Did you ever have a dog?"

She blinked. "I beg your pardon?"

He motioned to the file and the doodle on the side.

"You think that means something? Doesn't every little girl have a dog?"

"Did you?" Boone waited patiently for her to answer.

"No, all right? If you must know, we lived in a building much like this one. The landlord didn't allow dogs."

"Hank doodled a dog. A girl with a dog. So there must be more than this," he said, indicating the file.

She shook her head. "Talk about jumping to wild conclusions." She picked up the flashlight from where she'd left it lying on the desk, the beam lighting most of the room, and shone it on the single sheet in the file.

"Hank had his own system. He numbered the pages in each file, keeping a running tally. It was his idea of organization. If you look on the back of the file, it shows how many papers are in each file. That way you can tell if anything is missing."

"Your partner got his office broken into a lot?" Boone quipped.

"It's the nature of the business," she said offhandedly.

He turned the folder over. There was a one on the back. One sheet of paper inside. He looked up to see her headed for the door. "Wait a minute, where are you going?"

"Home to bed," she said, after picking up three file folders from the desk where she'd stacked them earlier.

"That's all you're taking? Aren't you even going to lock the office door?"

"What's the point?" she said over her shoulder. "If there was anything in here worth stealing, it's long gone now."

Taking the McGraw file, he went after her, catching up to her at the stairs. "Look, Ms. West—"

"C.J." She met his gaze. In the dim light of the naked bulb over the stairs, he noticed her eyes were a rich, warm brown, the same color as his favorite horse. "Yes?"

He realized he'd been staring. At least he had the sense not to voice his thoughts. He doubted she would appreciate her eye color being compared to that of his horse's hide even if it was his favorite. "You should at least have my phone number, don't you think?"

He started to reach for his wallet and his business card, but stopped when she smiled, a rather lopsided smile that showed definite amusement. "I already have it." Reaching into her pocket, she brought out his wallet.

"You picked my pocket?" He couldn't help the indignation in his tone. "What kind of private investigator are you?" he demanded, checking his wallet. His money and credit cards were still there. Now he knew what she'd been doing in the bathroom. All she'd apparently taken was his business card.

When he looked up, he saw pride glittering like fireworks in the rich brown of her eyes. "I'm the kind of PI who doesn't take anything at face value. I'm also the kind who doesn't work with amateurs, so this is where we part company. I'll call if I find out anything about your sister or the kidnapping." With that she turned and disappeared down the stairs.

He caught up with her at the street. "I'm not leaving town. If I have to, I'll dog your every footstep."

"As entertaining as that sounds—"

"I'm serious. I'll stay out of your way, but you can't keep me out of this."

She smiled as if she could and would and climbed into an older-model yellow-and-white VW van. The engine revved. He thought about following her to see where she lived. But he wasn't going to sit outside her residence all night to make sure she didn't give him the slip in the morning. He couldn't force her to help him anymore than he could make her keep him in the loop.

The woman was impossible, he thought as he climbed into his pickup and watched C.J. West drive away. A car a few vehicles away started up and left, as well. He glanced at it as it passed but didn't notice the driver. His mind was on C.J. West.

He knew nothing about her. She, he feared, knew everything about him, or would soon. The entire story of his family's lives for the past twenty-five years was on the internet.

Swearing, he reminded himself what was at stake. He couldn't go home without good news for his father. Hank Knight had started a file. He thought of the brief file now lying on the seat next to him. "Pink ribbon. Pink grosgrain ribbon."

It didn't take much of a mental leap to come up with a pink ribbon since Oakley's horse had a blue ribbon on it. If that information had gotten out, then... But pink grosgrain? Had their attorney Jim Waters released that information to the PI? Or had Hank already known about the toy stuffed horse and the key bit of information about the pink ribbon?

Now more than ever, Boone believed that Hank Knight had known something about the kidnapping. Had maybe even known where Jesse Rose was. Or at least suspected. And it might have gotten him killed.

One way or the other, Boone had no choice. He was staying in Butte and throwing in with this woman whether she liked it or not. He just hoped he wouldn't live to regret it.

Chapter Five

C.J. closed her apartment door and leaned against it for a moment. Tonight, being in Hank's office, she'd felt him as if he was there watching her, urging her on.

Tell me who killed you! she'd wanted to scream.

She hadn't been able to shake the feeling that he'd left behind a clue. Some lead for her to follow that even whoever had ransacked the office wouldn't get, but she would because she and Hank had been so close they could almost read each other's mind.

Until recently. Lately he'd been secretive.

But did it have something to do with the McGraw kidnapping? Just because she'd found the file in Hank's hiding place, it didn't mean it was the last case he was working on. While she and Boone had found a couple of recent case files, neither of them had seemed like something that could get Hank killed. Then again, like Boone had said, any case could turn violent.

She'd tossed the three file folders from fairly recent cases of Hank's on the kitchen table as she'd come into the apartment. Now she moved to them. Other than the McGraw file, there was one labeled Mabel Cross. Inside, she found a quick abbreviated version of Mabel's problem. The woman suspected that her niece had taken an antique brooch of hers. But she also thought her daughter's husband might have taken it. She had wanted Hank to find it and get it back.

The second file folder was labeled Fred Hanson. His pickup had been vandalized. He was pretty sure it was one of his neighbors since they'd been in a disagreement. He wanted to know which one of them was guilty.

The third case, Susan Roth Turner, suspected her husband might be having an affair.

C.J. sighed. None of those seemed likely to have gotten Hank killed. But she knew better than to rule them out since other than the McGraw file, they were his most recent cases and three of his last ones before he was to retire.

Moving to the refrigerator, she poured herself a glass of red wine and headed for the couch. This was the hardest part of her day. As long as she was busy taking care of all the arrangements for Hank's funeral, tying up loose ends with their business dealings and looking for his killer, she could keep the grief away.

But it was moments like this that it hit her like a tidal wave, drowning her in the pain and regret. Hank had taught her everything about the private eye business from the time she was old enough to see over the top of his big desk. Her mother had worked in the building back in those days and C.J. used to wander the halls, always ending up in Hank's office.

He'd pretended that her visits were a bother, but she'd known he hadn't meant it. He'd started bringing her a treat, an apple, a banana or an orange, saying she should have something healthy. He'd always join her, pushing aside a case file to sit down and talk with her. Even extinguishing his cigar so the smoke didn't bother her.

From the time she was little, she loved listening to him talk about the cases he was working on. He never mentioned names. But he loved discussing them with her. She had seen how much he loved his job, how much he loved helping people. He'd hooked her on the PI business. All she'd ever wanted was to be just like him.

Hank had loved it all, especially solving mysteries that seemed impossible to solve. He was good at his job and often worked for little or nothing, depending on how much his clients could afford.

Sometimes we're all a person has, he used to tell

her. *They need help and everyone else has turned them down.*

So how was it that he'd gotten himself killed?

Exhausted, still grief stricken and feeling as if she was in over her head, she wandered into the bedroom to drop onto the bed. She desperately needed sleep, but she picked up her laptop because she had a feeling she hadn't seen the last of Boone McGraw.

Within minutes she was caught up on the latest information that had been released to the press about the twenty-five-year-old kidnapping as well as what she could find out about Boone. The more she read about the kidnapping, the more she worried that he was right and Hank had discovered something about the case that had gotten him killed.

She didn't want to believe it. What could he have found out that had put him in such danger? She recalled something Boone had said and dug her cell phone out of the back pocket of her jeans.

"Can't sleep?" Boone said in answer to her call.

"You said something earlier about this Vance Elliot turning out not to be Oakley McGraw. He must have had some kind of proof to make you think he was the missing son."

"He had my little brother's stuffed horse."

She lay back on the bed. "What made you think it was the same horse?"

"It had a blue ribbon tied around it and some of

the stitching was missing. Oakley never slept without it in his crib."

"So how did he just happen to have this horse, if he wasn't the real Oakley McGraw?"

"It's a long story, but basically, someone had picked up the horse as a souvenir at the crime scene and later decided to use it to get money out of my father."

"So you have no idea who in the house helped the kidnapper take the twins? What about the nanny who became your stepmother? She seems the perfect suspect. I just read that she might be released from jail until her trial for attempted murder."

"Suspect, yes. But for trying to kill my father, not for the kidnapping."

Exhaustion pulled at her. She could hardly keep her eyes open. "So they were fraternal twins, right? Six months old." She was thinking of what Hank had written in the file. "I'm assuming your sister also had a stuffed horse toy in her crib that was taken that night? One with a pink ribbon."

"Yes."

She closed her eyes, seeing the yellow lined paper and the words *pink ribbon* written in Hank's even script. *Pink grosgrain ribbon*. "Was there anything about the ribbon around its neck released to the media?"

"No. There was nothing about it being a pink *grosgrain* ribbon."

"That's the kind that has the ridges, right? The lawyer must have mentioned it to Hank—"

"I'm sure he provided information about the kidnapping to Knight Investigations, but not that," Boone said. "Hank knew something before he made the call. Otherwise why would he have contacted our family lawyer with questions about Jesse Rose?"

Good question. Unfortunately, C.J. had no idea. But her gut instinct told her that Boone was right. Hank had already known all about the kidnapping twenty-five years ago. For some reason, he had followed the case closely all these years.

But if he'd kept anything in writing, she hadn't found it. Yet.

"I'm going to the police station in the morning to find out more about Hank's death," Boone said.

"Good luck with that." She hung up and rolled over, too tired to get undressed. And yet her thoughts refused to let her sleep.

Was there more information Hank had hidden somewhere? Why wasn't the information in the file? Because he knew enough to know he was in danger?

If this was about the McGraw kidnapping, had Hank gotten too close to the truth? But wouldn't that mean that he had inside knowledge? Wasn't the fear that Hank had inside information and that was what had her running scared now?

She rolled over on her back and stared up at the ceiling, her mind racing. Had Hank already known about the pink ribbon? Or had the attorney told him? Either way, Hank had written it down. He'd also told the attorney that he had to go out of town. But he hadn't. Or had he?

She thought of Boone McGraw. He'd seen the words *pink grosgrain ribbon* in Hank's scrawl. He'd known then that Hank knew more than he had told the lawyer. Why hadn't the cowboy said something then?

Because he was holding out on her. Just like she was on him.

She felt a shiver and pulled the quilt over her. If Hank had known where to find Jesse Rose, then he would have told the McGraw lawyer, she told herself. Unless…unless he had something to hide.

Her eyes felt as if someone had kicked sand into them. She closed them and dropped like a stone into a bottomless well of dark, troubled sleep.

THE NEXT MORNING, Boone stopped by the police station and after waiting twenty minutes, was led to a Detective Branson's desk. The man sitting behind it could have been a banker. He wore a suit, tie and wire-rimmed glasses. He looked nothing like a cop, let alone a detective.

As Boone took a seat, he said, "I'm Boone—"

"McGraw. Son of Travers McGraw. I know. You told my desk clerk. That's why you're sitting where you are when I'm so busy."

He was used to his father's name opening doors. "I'm inquiring about a private investigator by the name of—"

"Hank Knight. He's dead." He looked back at the stack of papers on his desk, then up again. He seemed surprised Boone was still sitting there.

"Can you tell me under what circumstance—"

"Hit-and-run. Given the time of night, not that surprising, and in front of a bar." The cop shrugged as if it happened all the time.

Boone could see why C.J. hadn't been happy after talking to the cops. "So you think it was an accident?"

Branson leaned back in his chair, his expression one of tired impatience even this early in the morning. "What else?"

"Murder."

The detective laughed. "Obviously you didn't know Hank or you wouldn't even ask that question. Hit-and-run accident. Case closed."

"Surely you're investigating it."

"Of course," Branson said. "Right along with all the other crimes that go on in this city. Why the interest?"

Boone could see that the hit-and-run was low priority. He thought about mentioning the kidnapping case. For twenty-five years anyone who heard the name would instantly tie it to the kidnapping. It had been a noose around his neck from the age of five.

"His partner believes it was murder."

"C.J. West?" He sneered as if that also answered his earlier question. The detective thought this was about him and the private eye?

"She has reason to believe it wasn't an accident," he said.

"PIs," Branson said and shook his head. "They just want to be cops. Trust me, it was an accident. So unless you know different, I have to be in court in twenty minutes…"

The detective went back to his paperwork. Boone rose. On his way out the door, he called C.J. on the number she'd called him from last night. "You were right about the cops."

"You doubted me?"

"My mistake." He could hear traffic sounds in the background on her end of the line.

"Think you can find the Greasy Spoon Café around the corner from the cop shop?" she asked.

Chapter Six

"You call this breakfast?" Boone McGraw said as he looked down at his plate thirty minutes later.

He'd had no trouble finding the small hole-in-the-wall café. This part of uptown Butte hung onto the side of a mountain with steep streets and over hundred-year-old brick buildings, many of them empty. The town's heyday had been in the early 1920s when it was the largest city west of the Mississippi. It had rivaled New York and Chicago. But those days were only a distant memory except for the ornate architecture.

"They're pasties," C.J. said of the meat turnover smothered with gravy congealing on his plate. "Butte is famous for them." She took another bite, chewing with obvious enjoyment. "Back when Butte mining was booming, workers came from around the world. Immigrants from Cornwall needed something easy to eat in the mines." She pointed at the pasty with her fork. "The other delicacy Butte takes credit for is the boneless deep-fat-fried pork chop sandwich."

"Butte residents don't live long, I would imagine," he quipped. "When in Butte, Montana…" He poked at the pasty lying under the gravy. It appeared to have meat and small pieces of potato inside. He took a tentative bite. It wasn't bad. It just wasn't what he considered breakfast.

He watched her put away hers. The woman had a good appetite, not that it showed on her figure. She was slightly built and slim but nicely rounded in all the right places, he couldn't help but notice. She ate with enthusiasm, something he found refreshing.

As he took another bite of his pasty, he studied her, trying to get a handle on who he was dealing with. There was something completely unpretentious about her, from her lack of makeup to the simple jean skirt, leggings, sweater and calf-high boots she wore. Her copper-red hair was pulled back in a loose braid that trailed down her back.

She looked more like an elementary school teacher than a private investigator. Because she was so slight in stature it was almost deceiving. But her confidence and determination would have made any man think twice before taking her on. Not to mention the gun he suspected was weighing down the shoulder bag she had on the chair next to her.

"What does the 'C.J.' stand for?" he asked between bites.

She wrinkled her nose and, for a moment, he thought she wasn't going to tell him. "Calamity Jane," she said with a sigh. "My father was a huge fan of Western history apparently."

"You never knew him?"

With a shake of her head, she said, "He died when I was two."

"Is your mother still…?"

"She passed away years ago."

"I'm sorry."

"Hank was my family." Her voice broke. Eyes shiny with tears, she looked away for a moment before returning to her breakfast. He did the same.

A few minutes later, she scraped the last bite of gravy and crust up, ate it and pushed her plate away. Elbows on the table, she leaned toward him and dropped her voice, even though the café was so noisy, he doubted anyone could hear their conversation where they sat near the doorway.

Her brown eyes, he noticed, were wide and flecked with gold. A faint sprinkling of freckles dotted her nose and her cheekbones. He had the urge to count them for no good reason other than to avoid the intensity of those brown eyes. It was as if she could see into him a lot deeper than he let anyone go, especially a woman.

"Tell me more about the kidnapping case," she said, giving him her full attention. "Don't leave anything out."

He took a drink of his coffee to collect his errant thoughts and carefully set down the mug. Last night she'd been so sure that the kidnapping case couldn't be what had gotten her partner killed. He wondered what had changed her mind—if that was the case.

"We all lived on the Sundown Stallion Station ranch, where my father raised horses. I was five. My older brother, Cull, was seven, Ledger was three. We had a nanny—"

"Patricia Owen, later McGraw after she became your father's second wife and allegedly tried to kill him," she said.

He nodded. "Patty stayed across the hall from the nursery. She heard a noise or something woke her. Anyway, according to her, she went to check on the twins and found them missing. When she saw the window open and a ladder leaning against the outside of the house, she started screaming and woke everyone up. The sheriff was called, then the FBI. A day later there was a ransom demand made. My father sold our prized colt to raise the money."

"Why wasn't the kidnapper caught when the ransom was paid?" she asked.

"The drop was made in a public place, but a fire broke out in a building close by. Suddenly the street was filled with fire trucks. In the confusion, some-how the kidnapper got away with the money with-out being seen."

She shook her head. "Who made the drop?"

"The family attorney, Jim Waters."

C.J. raised a brow. "Isn't he the one who was also arrested trying to leave the country with a bunch of money and has also been implicated in your father's poisoning?"

Boone nodded, seeing that she knew a lot more than she was letting on. "But so far no charges have been filed against him in the poisoning and there is no proof he was involved in the kidnapping. We now know that Harold Cline, a boyfriend of our cook, climbed the ladder that night and got away with the twins. The person who hasn't been found is the one who it is believed administered codeine cough syrup to the twins to keep them quiet during the ordeal and passed them out the window to the first kidnapper."

"What about the broken rung on the ladder?" she asked.

"It was speculated that the kidnapper might have fallen or dropped the babies, but we now know that didn't happen. The babies were alive and fine when they were found by our family cook and taken to—"

"The Whitehorse Sewing Circle member Pearl Cavanaugh. Wasn't she or her mother the one who started the illegal adoptions through this quilt group years ago?"

C.J. had definitely done her homework. He figured she must have been up before daylight. Either that or she had known more about the case than she'd led him to believe last night.

"That's right. Unfortunately, they're pretty much all dead, including Pearl."

"So there is no record of what happened to the twins," she said and picked up her coffee mug, holding it in both hands as she slowly took a sip.

"In light of what we learned from our family cook before she died, the babies probably went to parents who couldn't have children and were desperate," he said.

"I can't imagine how they couldn't have known about the kidnapping. So in their desperation, they pretended not to know that the child they were adopting was a McGraw baby? Didn't Oakley's and Jesse Rose's photos run nationally? So no one could have missed seeing them."

He nodded. "It makes sense that whoever got each of the twins knew. We've been led to believe that the adoptive parents were told the twins weren't safe in our house."

She put down her cup, her brown-eyed gaze lifting to his. "Because of your mother's condition."

He thought of his mother in the mental ward, the

vacant stare in her green eyes as she rocked with two dolls clutched in her arms. "We now believe that her condition was the result of arsenic poisoning. It causes—"

"Confusion, memory loss, depression... The same symptoms your father was experiencing before his heart attack. Patty's doing is the assumption? So you're saying your mother probably wasn't involved."

He met her gaze and shrugged. "In her state of mind at the time of the kidnapping, who knows? But she definitely didn't run down your partner. She's still in the mental ward. And neither did Patty, who is still behind bars."

C.J. bit at her lower lip for a moment. He couldn't help noticing her mouth, the full bow-shaped lips, the even white teeth, just the teasing tip of her pink tongue before he dragged his gaze away. This snip of a woman could be damned distracting.

"You said Oakley has been found?"

That wasn't information she could have found on the internet. "He has refused to take a DNA test, but my father is convinced that the cowboy is Oakley. He owns a ranch in the area. Apparently he's known the truth for years, but didn't want to get his folks into trouble. They've passed now, but he still isn't interested in coming out as the infamous missing twin. Nor does he have an interest in being a McGraw."

She raised a brow. "That must be both surprising and disappointing if it's true and he's your brother."

"It's harder on my father than the rest of us. He's been through so much. All he wants is his family together."

She said nothing, but her eyes filled before she looked down as the waitress came over to refill their coffee cups.

C.J. STUDIED BOONE while he was distracted with the waitress refilling his cup. She'd known her share of cowboys since this was Montana—Butte to be exact. Cowboys were always wandering in off the range—and usually getting into trouble and needing either a private investigator or a bail bondsman. She and Hank had been both.

But this cowboy seemed different. He'd been through a lot because of the kidnapping. He wasn't the kind of man a person could get close to. Last night she'd noticed that he didn't wear a wedding ring. This morning online, she'd discovered that only one of the McGraw sons, Ledger, the youngest one, had made the walk to the altar.

"You drove a long way yesterday," she said after a few moments. "Seems strange if all you had to go on was Hank asking a few questions about the kidnapping and Jesse Rose."

He pushed away his plate, his pasty only half-eaten. "I quizzed the attorney when he told me about the private investigator calling. Truthfully, I figured this whole trip would turn out to be a wild-goose chase."

"So why are you here?"

"Because my father asked me and because our attorney said that Hank Knight sounded...worried."

Her pulse quickened. *"Worried?"*

Boone met her gaze with his ice-blue one. "I think he knew something. I think that's why he's dead." When she didn't argue the point, he continued. "From what you found last night, we know that he knew more about the ribbon on the stuffed toy horse than has been released."

"Why would he keep that information to himself?" she asked more to herself than to him.

"Good question. He told our attorney that he had to take a trip and would be out of town," Boone reminded her. "Makes sense he'd want to verify what he was worried about, doesn't it?"

It did. "Except I don't think he left town."

"Or maybe he had a good reason not to want me following up on it."

She bristled. "Hank was the most honest man I've ever known. If he knew where Jesse Rose was, he would have told your family."

"Maybe. Unless someone stopped him first."

Chapter Seven

After he paid the bill, they stepped outside the café. The morning air had a bite to it although the sky was a cloudless blue overhead. He was glad he'd grabbed his sheepskin-lined leather coat before he'd left home. Plowed dirty snow melted in the gutters from the last storm. Christmas wasn't that far off. There was no way Butte wouldn't have a white Christmas.

"What do you know about Butte?" C.J. asked as she started to walk up the steep sidewalk.

He shook his head as he followed her, wondering why she'd called him. Was she going to help him find out the truth? Or was she just stringing him along?

"What most Montanans know, I guess. It's an old copper mining boomtown and we're standing on what became known as the Richest Hill on Earth," he said. "It is now home to the Berkeley Pit, the most costly of the largest Superfund sites and a huge hole full of deadly water."

He saw that she didn't like him talking negatively about her hometown and realized he would have taken exception if she'd said anything negative about Whitehorse, too.

"Why are you asking me about Butte? What does this have to do with Hank or—"

"Butte was one of the largest and most notorious copper boomtowns in the West with hundreds of saloons and a famous red-light district."

Butte hadn't lived down its reputation as a rough, wide-open town. He'd heard stories about the city's famous red-light and saloon district called the Copper Block on Mercury Street. Many of the buildings that had once housed the elegant bordellos still stood.

"The first mines here were gold and silver—and underground," she continued. "They say there is a network of old mine tunnels like a honeycomb under the city."

"Where are you going with this, C.J.?"

"Hank loved this town and he knew it like the back of his hand."

Boone often wondered how many people actually knew the back of their hand well, but he didn't say so. "Your point?"

"He believed in helping people. Often those people couldn't pay for his services, but that never stopped him. You've seen his office. He wouldn't have been interested in your family kidnapping case. It wasn't something he would have taken on."

"Then how do you explain the fact that he knew about the ribbon?"

"Maybe the attorney told him. Look, there was only one sheet of paper in the file. Hank might have been curious given the latest information that's come out about the kidnapping. But he wouldn't have pursued it. Which means if not an older case, then one of his more recent ones has to be what got him killed. I need to investigate those. I'm sure you have better things to do—"

He didn't believe her. All his instincts told him that she wanted him to believe Hank hadn't known anything about the kidnapping. She was scared that he had. And maybe even more afraid because he hadn't told her.

So she was going to chase a few of Hank's last cases? He'd seen her take three files last night. "Fine, but you aren't getting rid of me, because once you exhaust your theory, we're going to get serious and find out what Hank knew about the McGraw kidnapping and Jesse Rose."

"Fine, suit yourself. I'm going to visit Mabel Cross and see if her brooch has turned up."

Boone shook his head. "Seriously?"

"As Hank used to say, there are no unimportant cases." She headed for her VW van. He cursed under his breath, but followed and climbed in the passenger side. She was wasting her time and his. But he needed her help and antagonizing her wasn't going to get him anywhere, he told himself as he climbed into the passenger seat of her van.

"So we're going to pay a visit to these people?" he asked, picking up the three case files she'd taken from Hank's office last night as she slid behind the wheel. "Tell me we aren't going underground." He didn't want to admit that one of his fears was being trapped underground. The idea of some old mine shaft turned his blood to ice.

She laughed. "I'm afraid we are. So to speak," C.J. said and started the engine.

The buildings they passed were old, most of them made of brick or stone with lots of gingerbread ornamentation. He recalled that German bricklayers had rushed to Butte during its heyday from the late 1800s to the early 1920s.

Nothing about Butte, Montana, let you forget it had been a famous mining town—and still was, he thought as they passed streets with names like Granite, Quartz, Aluminum, Copper—and Caledonia.

As she drove C.J. waved or nodded to people they passed. He couldn't tell if she was just friendly or knew everyone in town. On Iron Street, she pulled to the curb, cut the engine and climbed out. As she headed for an old pink-and-purple Victorian, he decided he might as well go with her.

Glancing around the neighborhood, he took in

the historical homes and tried to imagine this city back in 1920. From photos he'd seen, the streets had swarmed with elegantly dressed residents. Quite a contrast to the homeless he'd seen now in doorways.

C.J. was already to the door and had knocked by the time he climbed the steps to the porch. The door opened and he looked up to find an elderly woman leaning on a cane. "Mrs. Cross," C.J. said. "I'm Hank Knight's associate."

"Hank." The woman's free hand went to her mouth. "So tragic. If you're here about his funeral—"

"No, I'm inquiring about your brooch. I wanted to be sure Hank had found it before—"

"Oh yes, dear," she said and touched an ugly lion studded with rhinestones pinned to her sweater. "Silly me. I feel so badly now to have thought my niece or my daughter's husband might have taken it and all the time it was on this sweater in the closet. I told Hank. I suppose he didn't get a chance to tell you before… He was so loved." She sniffed. "You'll be at his funeral, I assume."

"Of course. I'm just glad you found your brooch." C.J. turned and headed for the van.

Boone wanted to point out what a waste of time that had been, but one look at her face when she climbed behind the wheel and he bit his tongue. "When is the funeral?"

"Tomorrow afternoon." She started the van, biting

at her lower lip as if to stanch the tears that brimmed in her eyes.

As she pulled out on the street, he saw her glance in the rearview mirror and then make a quick turn down a side street. "So do we check on these other two cases?" he asked picking up the file folders.

"I already called Fred Hanson this morning. Hank got the neighbor to admit he did it and pay restitution."

Boone couldn't help being impressed. Who had this Hank Knight been to have such a devoted following, including C.J. herself?

"I also drove by the Turner house earlier this morning."

"The cheating husband case," he said.

"The husband's clothing was in the yard."

"Another case solved by Hank Knight. So are you ready to accept that he might have been involved in my family's case?"

She said nothing. On Mercury Street, she stopped in front of a large redbrick building and, cutting the engine, climbed out.

"The Dumas Brothel?" he asked, seeing the visitor sign in the window as he hurried after her.

"One of Hank's best friends works here," she said as she opened the door and stepped in.

He followed, wondering if she wasn't leading him

on a wild-goose chase this morning, hoping he'd give up and leave town.

It was cool and dimly lit inside the brothel museum. The older woman who appeared took one look at C.J. and disappeared into the back. Surely C.J. didn't plan on taking him on a tour.

But before he could ask, she turned and went to the front window. He could see her pain just below the surface and reminded himself that her partner had been killed only days ago. He didn't kid himself when it came to her priorities. She was looking for Hank's murderer—not Jesse Rose.

But if he was right, then it would lead them to the same place.

As he studied her, he couldn't help but wonder what she would do when she found the murderer.

An elderly man came into the room and C.J. turned and said, "Can we go out the back?"

Without a word, the man led them through the building and the next thing Boone knew, he was standing in a narrow alley surrounded by tall old brick buildings.

"What was that all about?" he demanded. He had expected her to at least ask the man about her partner or his death.

"Someone's following us," she said as she led him into another building, this one apparently abandoned.

A few moments later, they spilled out into a dark narrow alley. "This way."

Boone followed her through the alley between two towering old brick buildings before she dropped down some short stairs and ducked into a doorway. He stopped to look back and saw no one.

"Come on," she called impatiently to him.

He hurried down the steps as she opened a door with a key and he followed her inside another musty building. "Calamity—"

"C.J.," she snapped over her shoulder as she took a set of stairs that led upward. Only a little light filtered through the warbled old dust-coated windows as they climbed.

Four floors up, she stopped. He noticed that she wasn't even breathing hard although she'd scaled the stairs two at a time as if they really were being chased. Now, though, she moved across the landing to a door marked Fourth Floor. Motioning for him to be quiet, she opened it a crack and looked out.

Boone couldn't help but think she was putting him on. All this cloak-and-dagger stuff. Was it really necessary?

She motioned for him to follow her as she finally pushed open the door and headed down the long hallway, stopping short at the last door. From her bag, she pulled out a set of keys, pushed one into the lock and then seemed to hesitate.

"What?" he whispered, even though all the doors along the hallway were closed and he could hear nothing but the beat of his own heart.

C.J. shook her head, turned the key and pushed open the door. It didn't connect until that moment where they were and why she'd been hesitant to enter.

Past her he could see what appeared by the decor to be a man's apartment. There was a photo on one wall of a middle-aged Hank Knight and C.J. when she was about eight and had pigtails. Both Hank and C.J. were smiling at the camera. "You haven't been here since he was killed."

"No." She stepped in and, after a furtive glance down the hall, he followed, closing and locking the door behind them.

Chapter Eight

The first thing that hit her in Hank's apartment was the scent of cigar smoke. It lingered even though he'd quit smoking them some years ago. At work, he had taken up sucking on lemon drops. She'd often wondered if he'd done that for her because of how often she would end up at his office visiting with him about their cases.

Tears stung her eyes. She drew on her strength as she looked around the room. The door opened to a small kitchen and dining room. Past it was the living room, a dark curtain drawn over the only window. Beyond that was the bedroom and bath.

She'd only been here one other time. "I doubt there is anything here to find, but we can look." She hated that she'd brought Boone. But if the McGraw kidnapping had gotten Hank killed...

"I would think this is the logical place for your partner to keep information he possibly didn't want you or anyone else to see," Boone said, stepping past her and deeper into the apartment. "I meant to ask you last night. He didn't use a computer?"

"No." She glanced toward the kitchen sink. One lone cup sat on the faded porcelain. An old-fashioned brew coffeepot sat on one of the four burners on the stove. A half-eaten loaf of bread perched on an ancient toaster.

She moved to the refrigerator and opened the door to peer inside. A plate with a quarter stick of butter sat next to a half-empty jar of peach jam, Hank's favorite. The jam and butter shared space with two Great Falls Select cans of beer. Other than containers of mustard, ketchup and mayonnaise, there was a jar of dill pickles and one of green olives.

Closing the door, she felt Boone's impatient gaze on her.

"What are you looking for? Don't tell me you're hungry again," he said. Out of the corner of her eye, she saw him reach down to go through some magazines on the coffee table in front of the worn couch.

She didn't answer as she checked the garbage. Empty except for a clean bag. The Hank she knew was far from neat. The other time she'd been here, the garbage had been near full and there'd been toast crumbs on the counter, the butter dish next to them. Was Boone right about Hank either just coming back from somewhere—or getting ready to go somewhere?

"I think you'd better come see this," Boone called from the bedroom.

C.J. headed in that direction, half-afraid of what he'd found. When she looked through the door, she saw a beat-up brown suitcase open on the bed half-full of clothing. Stepping closer, she saw that Hank had packed two pairs of slacks and his best shirts.

She quickly glanced toward the closet, suddenly worried that he had planned to be gone longer than a few days. But most of his clothing was still hanging in the closet.

"What do you make of this?" Boone asked, eyeing her openly.

"He was either leaving or had just come back. His refrigerator is nearly empty and everything is cleaned up."

"So what he told my family lawyer might be true. He'd gone somewhere. To visit family?"

She shook her head. "He didn't have any family that I knew of." On top of that, Hank had hated to travel. In all the time she'd known him he'd left Butte only a couple times a year and always on a case—or so he had led her to believe. That she doubted his honesty now made her feel sick to her stomach.

She stepped to the suitcase to run her fingers along the fabric of one of the shirts. It was a gray-and-white-striped one she'd bought him for Christmas last year. He only wore it for special occasions. So what was the special occasion?

And why had he kept it from her?

BOONE COULD SEE C.J.'s confusion and hurt. Whatever her partner had been up to, he hadn't shared it with her. "I don't see a phone and he'd had the one at his office disconnected. I can see living off the grid, but..."

C.J. seemed to stir. Before that, she'd been staring into the suitcase, her thoughts dark from the frown that marred her girl-next-door-adorable face. "He recently bought a cell phone." Her frown deepened. "It wasn't found on his body."

Boone's pulse kicked up. "Was it possible someone took it off his body?"

Her brown eyes widened. "You mean someone in the crowd that must have gathered outside the bar?"

"We should search the rest of the apartment," Boone said, seeing how hard it was for her to keep her emotions at bay. He looked through drawers in the bedroom while she searched the bathroom and the living room.

"Something else is bothering me," he said when he found her going through a pile of old mail. "How was he planning to travel? I went through the suitcase but there wasn't a plane ticket in there. I suppose it could be an e-ticket on his phone."

She shook her head. "Hank wouldn't have flown. He always said that if God had wanted us to fly, He would have given us wings. He must have driven or been planning to."

"Where's his car?"

C.J. HAD BEEN so upset and busy with funeral arrangements and everything else that she hadn't been thinking clearly. It explained why she hadn't sent this cowboy packing. Like she'd told him last night, she didn't need or want his help. At least the latter was true.

"I hadn't even thought about his car. I just assumed that he'd walked down to the bar from here," she said. "He was hit in front of the bar. Now that I think about it, I didn't see his car parked where he usually leaves it."

"I think we should find it. What does he drive?" Boone asked as they left the apartment via the fire escape and ended up in another alley. The wind had picked up and now blew between the buildings, icy cold. A weak December sun did little to chase away the chill.

"A '77 Olds 88, blue with a white top."

"So where is this bar?"

"Not far." She thought of the bar owner and realized she should have gone to see him before this.

Natty would be as upset by all this as her. But then Hank had had so many friends.

A few blocks later, they entered the rear of the bar and she braced herself. This had been Hank's favorite bar. When he'd walk in the door, there would be a roar of greetings. Everyone had wanted to shake his hand and buy him a drink. But, never one to overindulge, he'd merely thank them and say he wasn't staying long.

As she started toward the front of the bar, C.J. half expected to see Hank on one of the stools. She thought of his face lighting up when he saw her and had to swallow back the lump in her throat and surreptitiously wipe her tears.

BOONE CAUGHT THE smell of stale beer and floor cleaner—like every Montana bar he'd ever been in. He'd grown to love the feel of them in college, but had been too busy on the ranch to spend much time on a barstool.

They went down a short hallway that opened into a dark room with a pool table. Ahead of them, he spotted a row of mostly empty stools pulled up to a thick slab of a bar. Only a little light filtered in through a stained-glass window, illuminating a scarred linoleum floor and a half dozen tables with empty chairs pulled up to them.

Following the sound of clinking glasses and the drone of a television, they reached the bar.

"What do you have against front doors?" Boone asked as C.J. headed for the bearlike man washing glasses behind the bar. When the grizzly bartender saw her, he quickly dried his hands and hurried around to draw her into a hug.

"How ya doin', sweetheart?" the man asked in a gravelly voice.

"Okay," C.J. answered. "I do have some questions, though, Natty."

The man called to one of the customers at the bar to hold down the fort and ushered them into an office down the hallway where they'd come in. Natty shot Boone a look, but C.J. didn't introduce either of them. On the wall, though, was a liquor license in the name of Nathaniel Blake.

"Did you see what happened or did anyone else we know?" she asked.

The man shook his head. "We just heard it. A couple of fellas went out to see what was going on." He looked as if he might cry. "I couldn't believe it."

"Did you talk to him before that?" she asked, her voice cracking a little. "I thought he might have mentioned where he was going."

Natty nodded. "I was surprised he was leaving again. He'd just gotten back. But he said he'd be gone for a few days and I knew what to do."

Boone saw her surprise and wondered at the man's words—*and I knew what to do.*

"Natty, he didn't tell me he'd left or that he was leaving again." She sounded close to tears and he wasn't the only one who heard it.

The big man put a hand on her shoulder. "He didn't tell me anything about it. But he hadn't looked happy about either trip. I wish I knew more. Whatever was going on with him, he wasn't saying."

She nodded. "You haven't seen his car, have you?"

"Matter of fact, it was parked across the street. I didn't think anything about it until I saw it being hauled off by the city. I would imagine it's down at the yard. Sorry, I should have called you, but I figured you had your hands full as it was."

She nodded. More sorry than the man could know, Boone thought. Everyone thought Hank's hit-and-run had been an accident. Everyone but his partner.

"I knew it was just a matter of time before you came by." He reached behind him, dug in a drawer for a moment and came out with an envelope. "I've been hanging on to this for you. Hank left it and said if anything should happen to him… I just thought it was because he was flying somewhere. You know how he felt about flying."

So he'd taken a flight. Boone could see that the news had astonished C.J.

"This last time, he said he was leaving town for a

while and didn't know when he'd be back, but I got the feeling he didn't think he was coming back. You think he knew?"

Knew that someone might try to kill him? Maybe, since he'd been in so much trouble that he hadn't wanted to share it with his partner, Boone thought.

Natty handed her the envelope. Even from where he stood, Boone could see that all it seemed to hold was a key. She undid the flap and took out the key. He saw that her fingers were trembling. There was a number printed on the key. 1171. He felt his pulse jump. Was this where Hank had hidden the information Boone desperately needed?

"You have any idea what that key opens?" Boone asked, worried that she might not.

Actually she did know, as it turned out. "It's to one of the lockers at the bus station."

His cell phone rang. He saw it was his brother Cull calling. "I need to take this. You won't—"

"I'll wait for you," she said, clearly upset from the news Natty had given her—and maybe the key, as well?

He stepped out of the office, but stayed where he could watch in case she tried to give him the slip. It wasn't that he didn't trust her… Oh, who was he kidding?

"Hello?"

"I was hoping we'd hear from you by now," his brother Cull said on the other end of the line.

"Afraid I haven't had much to report. It's been… interesting," Boone said.

"I know you didn't think much of Jim Waters's tip—"

"Actually, I'm beginning to think that there was something to it." He quickly told his brother about Hank Knight having been killed by a hit-and-run driver. "I'm hoping he left behind some information. It's why I'm working with Hank's partner to try to find it. What's that noise in the background?"

"Tilly vacuuming," Cull said, raising his voice to be heard. "Let me step into Dad's office."

"*Tilly*? I saw her the other day as I was leaving, but I thought she'd just come by to visit. Didn't she quit when Patty was arrested?"

"Yep," Cull said, the sound of the vacuum dying in the distance as his brother closed the office door. "Dad gave her a nice severance package for all the years she was our housekeeper, but apparently either it didn't last or she missed us."

"More than likely it's the new house," Boone said. "She always thought that the old one was haunted. I'm not surprised Dad took her back, though. I just hope she didn't let her ex get hold of her severance money. He kept her broke all the time. It was one thing after another with that guy."

"I doubt Tilly would want anything to do with him. When she needed him the most he ended up in the hospital after getting drunk and wrecking their car."

"Poor Tilly. I hope you're right about her being back because of the new ghost-less house."

"No ghosts yet anyway," Boone said under his breath.

"So what is this partner like? Does he think Hank's death had something to do with the kidnapping and Jesse Rose?"

"Not exactly. She's been skeptical at best but—"

"She?"

Just then C.J. came out of Natty's office saying her goodbyes.

"Is that her? She sounds *young.*"

Boone wasn't about to take the bait. "I'll call you as soon as I know something." He disconnected and followed C.J. out the back way of the bar again.

THEY WALKED THE few blocks to the bus station. A cold wind blew between the buildings. They passed a homeless man playing a pink kid's guitar. C.J. dropped a few dollars into the man's worn cowboy hat and he promised to play a song just for her.

After a few chords, they moved on, only to pass other homeless people who C.J. called by name. Each time, she gave them a few dollars and wished them well. Boone found himself enchanted with her generous spirit. Whitehorse didn't have homeless. Sure, a few passed through, spending a night in one of the churches, being fed by locals, but then they were on the road again.

The bus station was empty. Not even any buses in the enclosed cavernous parking area. The lobby had a dozen empty chairs. Past it were the restrooms and finally a hallway filled with old metal lockers.

"Why would Hank leave something here for you?" Boone asked. She had recognized the key so she'd either been here before or—

"When I was a girl, it was a game we played," she said as she pulled the key from her pocket. "He would hide things for me to find and give me clues. He said it was a good way for me to train if I really wanted to be a private investigator like him. I think he did it just to keep me busy and out of his hair and my mother's."

He watched her insert the key and turn it. The locker door groaned open. For a moment, he thought the space was empty. But C.J. reached into the very back and brought out another key, this one to a safety-deposit box.

Boone shook his head. "Are you sure he isn't just keeping you busy again?"

She cupped the key in her hand, her fingers closing over it. "The bank is only a few blocks away," she said, closing the locker and leaving the first key still in the door.

Back out in the fall sunlight, Boone took a breath. He was trying his best not to be irritated by all this cloak-and-dagger secrecy. He kept asking himself, what if Hank Knight's death *had* been nothing more than an accident?

Inside the bank, they were led to the back. C.J. had to sign to get into Hank's safety-deposit box. Apparently her name had always been on the list since they were quickly led into a room full of gold-fronted boxes. The bank clerk put her key into one, then took C.J.'s key and inserted it before she stepped away.

The moment they were alone, C.J. turned her key and pulled out the box. She carried it over to a table and simply stared at it.

"Aren't you going to open it?" he asked.

"I have a bad feeling I don't want to know what's in there."

"Want me to do it?"

She looked up at him with those big brown eyes and nodded.

He stepped closer and slowly lifted the lid, also worried that whatever was in there might devastate C.J. If Hank had been involved in the kidnapping in any way, he feared it would break her heart. Hank

Knight was a saint in her eyes. What would happen if she learned he was just a man—a man with a possibly fatal flaw?

Chapter Nine

C.J. wasn't sure how much more she could take. Hank had known he was in trouble. Otherwise he wouldn't have left the keys for her. Why hadn't he let her help him? Maybe he would still be alive if—

She heard Boone open the safety-deposit box, heard him make a surprised sound. Before that, she'd turned away, fighting for the strength she needed to face whatever Hank had left her. A confession? Something he needed her to hide?

"What is it?" she demanded now as she turned to Boone again.

He reached into the box and brought out the contents. He fanned some documents in front of her face.

"What are those?"

"Stocks and bonds, a whole hell of a lot of them. It appears he left you a small fortune."

She shook her head. "How is that possible? He barely made enough money to keep a roof over his head and what he did make, he gave away."

Boone laid the certificates on the table. "C.J., these are pretty impressive. Either he had a good stockbroker or he made more money than anyone thought he did or…" His gaze came up to meet hers. He lifted an eyebrow.

"He wasn't into anything illegal." She picked up one of the stock certificates and quickly put it down to look into the safety-deposit box. It was empty. No note. No explanation. Just a whole lot of questions she didn't want to ask herself.

"It appears that you were his sole beneficiary."

BOONE COULD TELL that C.J. was shaken. She put all the stock certificates back into the safety-deposit box and returned it, pocketing the key. He wanted to say something that might make her feel better. Hank Knight had left her a small fortune. She was rich. But clearly she wasn't happy about any of it.

Probably because it brought up the question of where Hank had gotten his money. On the surface, his life made it appear that he didn't care about money.

But the safety-deposit box proved that was a lie. Had Hank Knight been leading a double life? Had he been involved in something illegal? Not the kidnapping, since that money had been found before the first kidnapper had been able to split it with his accomplice. At least that was the theory.

But there still could have been a payoff. It's possible whoever had Jesse Rose had been forced to pay for her. It still didn't explain the amount of money Hank had left C.J., unless selling babies had been his real ongoing business.

Boone was half-afraid what else they would find. All he could hope was that this runaround would eventually lead to Jesse Rose.

He watched C.J. call the city on her cell. She hung up after apparently only reaching a recorded message. "They're closed today. I can't get his car out until tomorrow."

"What now?" Boone asked.

"There's someplace I need to go," she told him. She still looked pale. As strong as she appeared, he could tell that all of this was taking its toll on her.

Again she took to the alleys, working her way through the maze of old buildings overlooking the valley.

He couldn't help thinking of her as a child racing around this tired old city to find the clues Hank had left her. He'd trained her well. So why hadn't he told her what was going on? Wouldn't he know that his holding out on her would hurt her? Clearly he'd been trying to protect her. But protect her from what?

All Boone could figure was if Hank had been half the man C.J. thought he'd been, then he'd been in trouble and didn't want to bring her into it. He felt his heart drop at the thought that Hank had known where Jesse Rose was and had now taken that information to his grave.

Ducking into a tiny café stuck between two old brick buildings, Boone followed C.J. inside. She headed for a table, sitting down with her back to the wall as if wanting to watch the door. Were they really being followed? If so, she hadn't mentioned it again since this morning.

C.J. WATCHED BOONE glance behind him before the door closed. She could tell that he hadn't believed her about someone tailing them earlier. He thought she was putting him on, leading him around just to wear him out. She smiled to herself, thinking that might have been partly true earlier.

"What are we doing?" he demanded.

"*I'm* having lunch," she said glancing past him at the large window that looked out onto the street. She saw movement in the deep shadows next to one of the buildings. But who or whatever it had been was gone now.

"If your plan is just to try my patience or wear me down…"

"You know my plan. It's to find out who killed Hank. If it is because of your kidnapping case…" She didn't need to finish since Boone was smart. He'd hang in as long as he thought she might lead him to his kidnapped sister. Even if it was the last place she hoped Hank's trail would lead them.

Not that she didn't want him to find his sister and reunite his family, but not at the expense of Hank's reputation. If Hank was involved, she wouldn't be able to protect him. Whatever happened now, she had no choice but to do her best to find out the truth. Wasn't that what Hank had taught her?

With obvious reluctance, Boone took a seat across from her. What choice did he have? She was his only hope of finding out why Hank had contacted Jim Waters and they both knew it. Boone had said that he couldn't go home until he had answers. Even if it meant putting up with her. And vice versa.

A waitress appeared and, without even looking at a menu, C.J. ordered "the usual" for them both.

"A little presumptuous," he said. "Tell me we aren't having more of those pasty things."

She ignored him as she looked past his shoulder. He turned to follow her gaze to the street but like her seemed to see nothing of interest.

"Still pretending we're being followed?" he asked, turning back to her.

Her gaze shifted to him. In the light coming through the window, his eyes were a brilliant blue. The cowboy was too handsome for his own good. Not that he seemed to realize it, though. She wondered how many women had flirted with him to no avail.

"Why don't you have a girlfriend?" she asked.

Those blue eyes blinked in surprise. "Who says I don't?"

She chuckled at that.

"I've had girlfriends," he said defensively. "I also have a horse ranch to run with my brothers. My father—"

"Had a heart attack. I understand he's better."

"He is. What about you?"

"I'm fine."

"You know what I mean. You have a steady beau?" He didn't wait for her to answer. "I didn't think so. So what's *your* excuse?"

She shook her head to keep herself from telling him the usual line—too busy, not interested in the men who were interested in her, hadn't met the right one yet and all the other things she'd told Hank when he'd asked the same question.

"I'd think you'd have a string of girlfriends," she said, knowing she was only trying to distract herself from what they'd found in the safety-deposit box.

"And you'd be wrong."

"Why is that? Some girl break your heart? Make you swear off women?"

"No. Is that what happened to you? The quarterback in high school or some studious young man at college?"

Fortunately she was saved as the waitress came

back with two overflowing plates. Fried pork chops hung over the buns next to heaping piles of French fries. "I didn't want you to leave Butte without a pork chop sandwich and this place makes the best ones," she said.

He locked eyes with her. "I'm not leaving until I find out what your partner knew about Jesse Rose and the kidnapping."

C.J. was the first to look away. "Like I think I've mentioned before, I'd have a better chance of finding out the truth without you tagging along."

"Too bad. You're stuck with me."

She glanced out the window again. "Is there any reason someone would be following *you*?"

He laughed. "Seriously? *If* someone really is following us, why would they be after me?"

"I don't know," she said, holding his gaze for a moment before she picked up one of her French fries.

"Well?" He apparently wasn't letting her off the hook.

She took a bite, chewed, swallowed and said, "It's none of your business."

"Aha! There *was* some boy." He laughed again. "I would think it's hard to find a man willing to date a woman who carries a gun in her purse."

C.J. smiled at that, seeing that he was trying to get a rise out of her. "You know so little about women— and men—it seems." She picked up her pork chop sandwich and took a bite. No simple task given the size of it.

He sighed, picked up his and took a big bite. She saw his expression and hurriedly swallowed before she laughed.

"You like, huh?"

HE LIKED, BOONE thought as their gazes met and held for a long moment. He liked the sandwich. He liked her—a lot. The more he was around her... He looked away first.

They'd just finished their lunch when his cell phone rang. He stepped outside the door to take the call. But he stayed where he could see C.J. He suspected she wanted him around now even less. The things they were finding out about her deceased partner weren't things she wanted anyone else to know—maybe especially him.

"One of those string of women after you?" C.J. asked when he returned to the table after assuring his father he'd call as soon as he knew something.

"My father. After my brother Cull told him about your partner being killed in a hit-and-run, he was worried about me."

"He should be," she said. "Someone has been following us all day."

WHEN THEY LEFT the café, C.J. took them out the back door. Boone's father was worried about him. She was, too. She didn't want to get Travers McGraw's son killed. That's why she knew she should stop this now.

She knew she could get rid of this cowboy without much effort. He didn't know Butte and she did. But she had to admit, there were moments when she didn't want to be alone. Sometimes, she thought, remembering the way he'd devoured his pork chop sandwich, she enjoyed his company. He kept her mind off Hank and the pain of his death.

But the more she learned about Hank, the more worried she was becoming. Where had he gotten all that money for the stocks and bonds? Had he known something about the kidnapping? About Jesse Rose?

She was still shocked and shaken by what she'd discovered at the bank. It was one thing for Hank to be going somewhere without telling her, but all that money... It was as if she'd never known the man. Like the clothes in the suitcase.

Hank hated dressing up. She hadn't even known that he owned a suit. He was as bad as she was when it came to dressing casually for their work. Most of the people they saw couldn't afford to hire a private investigator. They dressed so they fit in with the community since Hank had never been interested in taking what he called highbrow cases.

Let some other PI take care of the rich, he'd always said. *We'll take care of the little guys, the ones who need us the most.* And she'd felt the same way.

It's called giving back to the community, Hank told her the first time she realized he didn't make much money. *People need help. If I can help, I do. This job isn't about the money.*

She'd seen right away how kindhearted the man was. He'd taken her on to raise, hadn't he? The only way C.J. had kept a roof over their heads once she'd become his partner was by taking insurance fraud cases while Hank continued to help those who couldn't help themselves.

That's why she'd been so sure Hank's death couldn't have had anything to do with the McGraws. It wasn't the kind of case that interested him. It was highbrow *and* high-profile. A wealthy horse ranch family. And yet, she'd found the file. She knew that Boone wouldn't lie about Hank talking to his family lawyer. But why?

And did the case have anything to do with Hank's hit-and-run? How about all that loot in the safety-deposit box? It made no sense given the way Hank had lived.

As they came out on the street, she glanced back. She hadn't spotted the tail since before lunch. All she'd caught was a shadowy figure lurking not quite out of sight. Why follow her to start with? Because they were afraid she would find out the truth?

"I should have gone to the restroom back at the café," C.J. said. "I'm going to duck in here."

"I'll wait out here for you," he said after glancing into the Chinese restaurant. He watched her go inside and disappear into a door marked Women. The air was brisk this afternoon, especially in the shade. He stomped his feet to keep them warm as he looked up the street toward the Berkeley Pit. What had once been a large natural bowl sitting high in the Rockies straddling the Continental Divide was now an open pit that stretched over a mile wide. It had become a tourist attraction, he thought with a shake of his head.

He glanced inside the restaurant. The door to the women's restroom was ajar. There was no sign of C.J. Even before he went inside and saw the rear entrance, he knew she'd given him the slip.

Chapter Ten

C.J. couldn't believe that she felt guilty about losing Boone McGraw. There was someplace she needed to go without him. When she was a girl and Hank was teaching her the PI business from the ground floor up, as he liked to call it, he would leave her messages in an old building uptown. She had looked back on those days, thinking it was charming, the cute things he came up with to keep her busy and out of his hair.

It had been years since he'd left anything for her at this particular place, but after everything that had happened, she felt she needed to check it.

And check it without Boone. He'd already learned too much about her and Hank. She was sure by now that he thought Hank had been dirty—how else could all those stocks and bonds at the bank be explained? That he'd saved that much from his PI practice? Not a chance.

She couldn't stand the thought of an investigation into Hank because of her. Boone swore that all he was interested in was finding his sister. She prayed that was true. Still, she thought as she walked the last block to the old building, she couldn't have Boone tagging along. Not right now. Hank had been in trouble or he wouldn't be dead right now, no matter what the police thought.

The building was abandoned like so many in Butte. She was just glad to see it still standing. One of these days it would either crumble and fall down or someone would come along and tear it down. Her heart ached at the thought of the memories that would go with it—not to mention the beautiful structure it had once been.

She climbed the steps to the wide double doors, now chained and padlocked, then stepped into the alcove to the right. At one time, there had been a fountain with water sprouting from the mouth of the ancient-looking stone face. But that had been years before C.J. herself. For as long as she could remember, the mouth had been dry like the bowl shape under it.

Today there were leaves and garbage in the bowl that used to catch the fresh water. She wished she'd brought a bag so she could clean it out, then reminded herself why she was there. She couldn't save this place. She wasn't even sure she could save herself if Boone was right and she was Hank's beneficiary. If her partner in business had gotten all that money from something illegal…

Reaching into the mouth, she felt grit and nothing else. Then her fingers brushed something cold. She touched it tentatively before she pulled out the small package. It was wrapped in plastic.

Seeing it, she began to cry. Hank knew her so well and vice versa. With trembling fingers, she saw the thumb drive protected inside the plastic cover and stuffed it into her pocket, her heart in her throat.

AFTER CUSSING AND carrying on for a while, Boone drove down random streets looking for her. Clearly there was someplace she'd wanted to go without him. Or maybe she'd just wanted to be alone.

That thought struck him hard. He'd seen how upset she'd been after finding the stocks and bonds at the bank. Didn't it make more sense to give her some space? He pulled over, parked and spent the next hour learning as much as he could about PI Hank Knight and his partner.

Everywhere he went, he heard nothing but praise about Hank and respect for C.J. The two were well-known around town as do-gooders. People liked them. People had been helped by them.

So where had all that loot come from? Hank had to be into something illegal. Perhaps a baby ring. The thought that Jesse Rose could have been one of the babies set his teeth on edge. C.J. knew more than she was telling him. Once he found her again…

He'd just driven down one of the main streets in uptown Butte, when he spotted her VW van and went roaring after her, riding her bumper. He cursed himself as C.J. whipped across two lanes of traffic on Montana Avenue and came to a tire-screaming stop at the curb. Before he could pull in behind her, she was already out of her van and storming toward him.

"What do you think you're doing?" she demanded.

He wished he knew. He wanted to throttle this woman or kiss her. Right now, he wasn't sure which and that said a lot about his frustration.

"I have no idea what I hope to accomplish by hanging around Butte—let alone tailing a junior PI who can't investigate her way out of a paper bag."

Hands on her hips, she glared at him. "What did you just call me? A junior PI who can't investigate her way out of a paper bag?" she demanded indignantly.

"Prove me wrong. Help me find my sister."

She glared at him for a full minute. "I told you what I'm doing. Trying to find my partner's killer."

"How are you doing on that?"

C.J. narrowed her eyes at him. "There is one more place I need to look. I'm assuming you plan to come along?"

"You're assuming right. We walking or taking my truck?"

She looked as if she could spit nails. "We're taking my van since you don't know where we're going." With that, she spun on her heel and headed for her van. He took a few deep breaths himself before following her.

Once behind the wheel with the van engine revved, she peeled out into the street and roared down the hill. Uptown Butte was a rollercoaster of steep streets. After a few blocks, she swung into a parking spot in front of one of Butte's historic buildings.

He climbed out after her and headed for the front door. C.J., he realized belatedly, was headed down the alley between the two buildings. The alley was just wide enough to walk down. It was cool and dark.

"Where—"

"If you're determined to tag along," she said over her shoulder, "then no questions."

Halfway down the long alley, she stopped at an old weathered padlocked door. Pulling out a set of keys, she opened the padlock and swung the door open.

Boone peered down a dark narrow concrete hallway, a musty, dank smell wafting out. He didn't like the looks of this.

"Close the door behind you," she ordered and stepped in.

He hesitated but only a moment before following her. Their footsteps echoed on the damp concrete. The smell got much worse as the passage became more tunnel-like.

She made a sharp right, then a left, then another right. He tried to keep track, telling himself he might need directions to get out of here. It crossed his mind that she might be leading him into a trap. If she and her partner were in league…

Boone realized that he'd lost track of the twists and turns. He was screwed if he had to get out of here by himself. If he was that lucky.

C.J. stopped and he almost crashed into her in the dim light. He heard the jingle of keys again. "Hold this," she ordered as she dug a flashlight from her shoulder bag and handed it to him.

He held the light on another padlock and few seconds later, she was entering yet another narrow passage.

"Where the—" He didn't get the rest of the words out as she turned on him.

"Shh," she snapped and was off again.

He had no choice but to go with her. If he thought she'd been leading him on a wild-goose chase earlier, he'd been wrong. But this definitely felt like she was fooling with him.

The next padlock opened into a room filled with

file cabinets. She flipped on a light switch and for a moment he was blinded by the overhead bulb.

C.J. had stopped just inside the door.

"What?" he asked.

"Hank didn't leave anything in here."

He stared at her. "You haven't even looked."

"Come on," she said, turning and starting for the door.

"No, wait, we came all this way, why not—"

"The dust."

"What?"

"Didn't you notice the dust on the floor?"

He couldn't say he had.

"Hank hasn't been in that room in months."

"Based on a little dust."

She glared at him in the ambient glow of the flashlight. "I'm just a junior PI who can't investigate my way out of a paper bag, but yes, that's my conclusion. I don't just jump to conclusions without facts."

"Really? And why all this subterfuge? What was it your partner did that he not only had to hide his files, but that he made a ton of money from?"

She gave him an impatient look before turning and heading down a different tunnel than the one they'd come in from. She had the flashlight. He had no choice but to follow her.

They came to a narrow stairway that wound up

a couple of stories and the next thing he knew they were standing outside in the sunlight.

He glanced around, trying to get his bearings. The tall brick buildings that had rivaled New York City now just looked sad, so many of them empty. They had come out not that far from the Berkeley Pit, a huge hole that was now full of bad water. Butte was now the butt of jokes, a decaying relic of better times.

"I don't know where else to look," she said, sounding disheartened. "I need a hot shower. You aren't going to insist on coming along for that, are you?"

It was late afternoon. The sun had sunk behind the mountains to the west. Dark shadows fell across the streets and a cold wind whipped between the buildings. Butte had fallen on hard times, especially the old uptown, and yet there was a quiet elegance to it. He wished he had seen it during its heyday. He was feeling a little nostalgic and disheartened himself.

"I'm sure it is all going to make sense at some point," he said.

Her smile was sad. She looked close to tears. He wanted to take her in his arms. But if he did, he knew he'd kiss her. He realized looking at her now that she had a bow-shaped mouth that just begged to be kissed.

"A hot shower sounds great. Back at my motel," he added, thinking a cold one might even be called for. "If you wouldn't mind dropping me at my truck."

BACK AT HER HOUSE, C.J. closed and locked the door behind her. She kept thinking of Boone. For a moment back there on the sidewalk, the sun slanting down through the buildings, she'd thought he was going to kiss her.

She shook her head now, telling herself she was tired and discouraged and scared. Boone wanted just one thing from her: answers.

Her hand went to her pocket and closed around the thumb drive Hank had left for her. She feared he'd left her answers—and she wasn't going to like them.

Taking off her jacket, she tossed it aside and picked up her laptop. Popping it open, she slid in the thumb drive, all the time praying she wasn't about to read Hank's confession.

What came up was even more shocking.

The photo was of a beautiful young dark-haired woman with the greenest eyes C.J. had ever seen. She was much prettier than the digitally enhanced photos that had run in the news showing what Jesse Rose McGraw would look like now. The young woman was smiling at the camera, eyes bright, as if whoever was taking the photo had said something funny.

She looked quickly to see what else was on the thumb drive, but there was only the one photo. She stared at Jesse Rose McGraw, her heart pounding. Hank had definitely known something about Jesse Rose.

But did it mean he'd been involved in the kidnapping? Or had he found out about Jesse Rose only recently? That was the question, wasn't it? The fact that he'd inquired with the McGraw family attorney gave her hope that he'd only recently stumbled onto the truth.

So why hadn't he told the attorney? Or at least called Travers McGraw and told him where he could find his daughter? It wasn't like Hank to keep a secret like that. So what had held him back?

It was the thought of what had stopped Hank from telling the McGraws the truth that had her running scared. Hank had been hiding something, there was no doubt about that. But what had kept him from doing the right thing?

C.J. closed the file, pulled out the thumb drive and pocketed it, her hands shaking. Hank had kept this from her and now she was about to do the same thing with Boone McGraw.

But she couldn't throw Hank under the bus. She had to know how he was involved—if he was. She had to find out where he fit into all of this. And then she would turn over this thumb drive. But until then…

AFTER A HOT SHOWER, followed by a cold one, Boone had gone over everything that had happened that day. None of it made any sense. The only conclusion he'd reached—and one he figured C.J. had, too—was that Hank was dirty.

That made him sad for C.J. Everything he'd learned about the two private investigators, though, was at odds with that conclusion. He'd seen C.J.'s reaction to the stocks and bonds in the safety-deposit box. She'd been dumbfounded. Which meant she had to be devastated by what they'd discovered today.

The question was, though, how did it tie in with the kidnapping and Jesse Rose? If it did at all.

He pulled out his cell phone and called C.J. "I need a drink after a day spent with you. What do you say to joining me?"

"A drink?"

He heard something in her tone. "Look, I don't have to get you drunk to hit on you, which I'm not, but if I was, I'd just back you up against a wall and—"

"Until you felt my gun in your ribs."

He laughed at the image. "Yes. Just so there is no misunderstanding, let's have dinner. We both have to eat. Or you don't even have to eat. You can just watch me."

She sighed and he thought for sure she was going to turn him down. To his surprise, she said, "There's a steakhouse close to your motel. I'll meet you there. Order me a steak, medium rare."

"Wait, you don't know where I'm stay—" He realized she'd already hung up. Of course she knew where he was staying. He could only guess how she knew. She'd probably followed him last night. He'd been too distracted to notice. He regretted what he'd said to her earlier about not being able to investigate her way out of a paper bag.

BOONE HADN'T BEEN waiting long when C.J entered the steakhouse. She looked a little out of breath as she slid into the opposite side of the booth. She'd told him to order for her and he had.

"I guessed baked potato loaded and salad with ranch dressing," he said.

She cocked a brow as she slid into the booth across from him. "I can live with that. What did you order?"

"The same." There was something different about her, he thought as he studied her. He got the impression that she'd walked here. Which meant she must not live far away. Either that or she'd needed the walk in the cold air.

She'd changed clothes and now wore a blouse and slacks, and her hair was tied at the nape of her neck. It cascaded down her back in a fiery river against the light-colored blouse. Silver earrings dangled from each ear and it appeared she'd applied lip gloss.

Something told him that none of this was about him. She seemed to wear all of it like armor as if she were going to war, reminding him that she was a private investigator first and foremost—and a woman on a mission. That they might not be on the same mission was still a possibility he had to accept.

He studied her, feeling a pull stronger than gravity. "I'm sorry about what I said to you earlier, you know, about the paper bag."

She smiled. "I'm sorry about dumping you earlier."

"It gave me time to do some investigating on my own," he told her, making her raise a brow. "I found out a lot about you and your partner."

"Really?" She seemed intrigued by that—and maybe a little worried. "All bad?"

"Actually, all good. The two of you are considered saints in this town."

She shook her head, almost blushing as she picked up her napkin and dumped her silverware noisily on the table. There was a tenseness to her tonight that he also didn't think had anything to do with him. After what they'd discovered at the bank, he'd seen how thrown she'd been. Had she found out even more to shake her faith in her partner?

"How was your time without me?" he asked.

"Pleasantly quiet." She smiled, though.

"I thought you might have missed me," he said.

She chuckled at that and carefully straightened her silverware. As the waitress brought their salads, C.J.

looked eternally grateful for something to do with her hands.

It surprised him to see her so nervous. Was it because she was having dinner with him, almost like a date? Or had something happened this afternoon after she'd dumped him that had her even more upset?

"So you talked to people about Hank?"

"And about you. Both of you are highly respected around town," he said when she didn't ask.

"That's nice. Anything else?"

"No one confessed to killing him, if that's what you're asking."

She nodded and dove into her salad as if she hadn't eaten in a week.

"So what *did* you do without me?" he asked, studying her.

"Just tying up loose ends," she said without looking up.

"You're sure that's all?"

She glanced at him, those warm, honey-brown eyes meeting his. He saw defiance along with something that made his chest ache—fear. C.J. was running scared. He got the feeling that didn't happen often.

"Do we have to talk business?" she asked.

"Is that what I was doing?" He took a bite of his

salad. What the devil had C.J. found out? And why meet him tonight if she wasn't going to tell him?

Their steaks came as they finished their salads. They ate without talking. He was hungry and quickly put away his steak and potato. Considering everything he'd eaten today, it seemed impossible. Must have been the high altitude of Butte that had him so ravenous. Or maybe it was a different kind of hunger that he was making up for.

As he pushed his plate away, he looked at C.J. She put her last piece of steak in her mouth, closed her eyes and chewed slowly.

"I take it you liked your dinner?" he joked, noticing that she'd eaten everything. "You're welcome to lick the plate."

She opened her eyes and swallowed. "I'm sorry you wasted the trip to Butte. There really isn't any reason for you to stick around tomorrow. I can get a friend to take me down to pick up Hank's car. If something else comes up, I know where to contact you."

There wasn't anything to say except, "Dessert?"

As she devoured a large slice of cheesecake, he had to wonder where she put it. She couldn't eat like this all the time. Then again, she probably had the metabolism of a long-distance runner.

"Thanks for dinner," she said after he'd paid and

walked her outside. It was dark with a cold breeze coming out of the mountains.

"I'm taking you home," he said, looking down the street to see several homeless men arguing.

"That isn't necessary."

"I'm afraid it is." He opened the passenger side of his truck and waited. He could see her having a private argument with herself, but she finally relented and climbed in.

He went around and climbed behind the wheel. Whatever she'd considered telling him tonight, she'd apparently changed her mind. Why else have dinner with him? Or maybe she'd just been hungry and he was buying.

"Just tell me where to go," he said as he started the pickup.

"Don't tempt me."

He looked over at her. "I'm going to take a wild guess here. This afternoon you found out something even more upsetting about Hank, but you don't want to tell me. In fact, it's why you gave me the slip earlier today. You're running scared that not only am I right about what got Hank killed, but that he is involved somehow in the kidnapping."

She looked out the side window and for a moment, he thought she might get out of the truck. Finally, she turned back to him. "Isn't it possible I'm just exhausted and have enough to deal with without you?"

He nodded. "But you agreed to have dinner with me. I was watching you while you ate. I could see that you were debating telling me something."

C.J. laughed. "You've never been very good at reading people, have you?" She looked out the windshield. "I live up that way."

He put the truck into gear and started in the direction she indicated. "I'm not leaving tomorrow. I'm going with you to the city car lot to get Hank's vehicle. If you don't want to go together, then I'll simply be waiting there for you."

"Turn left up here," she said. "Then right at the light." They were headed up the mountain to an area he'd been told was called Walkerville. The street went straight up through smaller and smaller, less ornate houses until she told him to turn right.

Her house was the last one on a short street that ended in a deep gully.

"Here," she said and the moment he slowed opened her door to get out.

"What time should I pick you up in the morning?" he asked.

In the cab light that came on as she climbed out, he saw her smile. "Are you always this pigheaded?"

"Always."

"Ten."

"I think you mean nine," he said before she could

close the door. "That is when the city lot opens and when you're planning to be there, isn't it?"

She smiled. "Nine, then," she said, and slammed the door.

THE NEXT MORNING, he was sitting outside C.J.'s house. Walkerville in the daylight looked even more like an old mining community up on the mountain overlooking the city. As she came out of the house, he climbed out of his pickup and went around to open the passenger-side door for her.

"I was hoping you'd left town," she said, clearly not pleased to see him.

"I almost did."

"What stopped you?" she asked as she climbed in.

"You," he said and shut her door.

As he slid behind the wheel, C.J. asked, "Could we make one stop first on the way? It's uptown. The city yard is down in the valley, so it isn't out of your way."

"Not a problem. I'm all yours. So to speak," he added and started the truck. "Sleep well?" he asked as he drove down the steep narrow streets.

"Fine." He glanced over at her. If she'd gotten any sleep, he would have been surprised. There were dark shadows under her eyes.

"I slept fine, too." Not that she'd asked.

She ignored his sarcasm as she gave directions to

where she wanted to go. "Right here," she said and the moment he stopped, she was out of the pickup and heading into another large brick building in the seedier part of town.

He cut the engine, parked and got out to follow her. Today she wasn't getting rid of him as easily as yesterday. But the moment he pushed open the door, he saw her in the arms of a large older woman. The two were hugging. He couldn't hear what was being said—no doubt condolences. He reminded himself of C.J.'s recent loss.

Boone felt a stab of guilt. He'd been so wrapped up in finding out what Hank had known about the kidnapping and Jesse Rose that he hadn't given a lot of thought or compassion to C.J. Maybe she was right and Jesse Rose and the kidnapping had nothing to do with Hank's death. Given the amount of money in those stocks and bonds, Hank could have been into something more dangerous than kidnapping.

He heard the older woman say, "I'm sorry, but I hadn't seen Hank in a few weeks. He didn't say anything about leaving town. Not to me."

"And he didn't leave anything for me?" C.J. asked, her voice rough with emotion.

The older woman shook her head. "I'm so sorry."

C.J. brushed at her tears and stiffened her back as the woman looked past her to where Boone was standing. Apparently neither had heard him enter.

"Thank you," C.J. said. She turned toward him but she didn't look at him as she made a beeline for the door.

He had only a second to get the door open and follow her out before she was on the curb. "I didn't mean to intrude just now."

Before she could answer, he heard the squeal of tires and the roar of an engine. The car came out of the alley at high speed. He didn't have time to catch more than the general shape and color of the car before it headed straight for C.J.

Chapter Eleven

It happened so fast that C.J. didn't have a chance to react. One moment she was standing at the curb, the next she was shoved aside and knocked to the ground with Boone McGraw crushing her with his body and the thick smell of engine exhaust wafting over them.

"Are you all right?"

She groaned as he rolled off her. The sound of the car engine died off in the distance. She became aware of people on the street huddled around them. "Did anyone get a plate number on that car?" she demanded as she tried to get to her feet.

Boone was on his. "Are you sure you're all right?" he asked, sounding a little breathless as he hunkered down beside her.

She nodded, though her knee was scraped and her wrist was hurt, but wasn't broken. She let him help her to her feet. She was more shaken than she'd thought when she was on the ground. One look at the people huddled around them and she could tell how close a call it had been. They were saying the same thing she was thinking. If it hadn't been for the cowboy...

If it hadn't been for Boone, it would have been another hit-and-run. Immediately, she thought of Hank. He hadn't had anyone to throw him out of the way. Could it have been the same car?

"A license plate number," she said to the small crowd around them again. "Anyone get it or a description of the car?" There was a general shaking of heads. Several said it had happened too fast.

"Kids," one woman said. "They could have killed you."

It hadn't been kids. Her every instinct told her that. It was too much of a coincidence that Hank had been run down and now she had almost been killed by a speeding car, as well.

She finally looked at Boone. He appeared even more shaken than she was. She saw that he'd pulled out his phone. "What are you doing?" she asked as the crowd began to disperse.

"Calling the cops."

"To tell them what? Did you see the car?" She saw that he hadn't gotten a look at it, either, before he'd thrown them both out of the way. "Even if they took it seriously, we don't have any information to give them. They'd just say it was another accident."

He hesitated for a moment before he pocketed his phone. "You're sure you're all right?"

She nodded, although still trembling inside. In all the years she'd been around and in the private investigation business, that was the closest she'd come to being killed. She'd been scared a few times, especially when caught tailing a person in a fraud case. But this was something new.

Which was probably why Hank hadn't seen it coming, either.

Boone opened the passenger side of his pickup and helped her in. She knew he was just being a gentleman because he felt guilty for still hanging around, but it made her feel weak and fragile—something she abhorred. She'd always had to be strong, for her mother. Now she had to be strong because otherwise she would fall apart. Hank was gone and she was terrified to find out why.

"You still think Hank's death has nothing to do with Jesse Rose and the kidnapping?" he asked as he started the pickup.

She didn't answer, couldn't. Her heart was lodged in her throat. Someone had just tried to kill her and would have taken Boone with her as she realized how close a call that had been. Worse, after looking at what was on that flash drive, there was no doubt. Hank knew something about Jesse Rose—and possibly her kidnapping.

Last night, she hadn't been able to sleep. She'd moved through her small house, restless and scared. At one point she thought she heard a noise outside. She'd never been afraid before living here. She'd always felt safe.

She'd checked all the doors and windows to make sure they were locked. But looking out into the darkness, she'd thought she'd seen the shape of a man in the trees beside the house. As she started to grab her purse and the gun inside, she saw that it was only shadows.

Her fears, she'd told herself, weren't any she could lock out. Hank had known about Jesse Rose. So why hadn't he told the McGraws?

Boone started the car. "Any other stops?"

She shook her head. "Let's go to the city lot and get Hank's car." With luck, he would have left something in it for her, not that she held out much hope. Hank's car always looked as if he was homeless and living in it. Finding a clue in it would literally be like looking for a needle in a haystack.

A FEW BLOCKS AWAY, Cecil pulled over to the side of the road. His hands were shaking so hard he had to lie over the wheel as he tried to catch his breath.

That had been so close. Just a few seconds later and he would have hit them both. Killed them both. He would have killed Boone McGraw. Killing some old PI was one thing. Even killing his young female partner. But if he had killed a McGraw…

The shaking got worse. He held on to the wheel as if the earth under him would throw him off if he didn't. And yet a part of him felt such desperate disappointment. He had to end this. C.J. West wasn't going to stop. He had to kill her. He had no choice.

When had things gotten so complicated? It had started out so simply and then he'd been forced to kill the PI. Now he would have to kill the PI's partner. As long as he didn't kill a McGraw. Travers McGraw would have every cop in the state looking for him if he did.

He began to settle down a little. He wouldn't get another chance, not with a hit-and-run. She would be expecting it now—and so would Boone. No, he'd have to think of something else. He knew where she lived.

An idea began to gel. Kill her and he should be home free.

Wiping the sweat from his face with his sleeve, he pulled himself together. He was steadier now, feeling better. He could do this. He could make up for his past mistakes. His head ached. He felt confused. There wasn't any other way out of this, was there?

He started to pull out, jumped at the sound of a loud car horn. A truck roared past, the driver flipping him the bird as he continued to lean on the horn.

Heart pounding, he checked his side mirror before slowly pulling out. He'd messed up, but he could fix it. He had no choice. But even as he thought it, he wondered how many more people he would have to kill to keep his secret. In for a penny, in for a pound, he thought.

Boone drove to the city yard and waited while C.J. went in to get Hank's car released. He still hadn't calmed down after their near miss back uptown. He would have loved to have passed it off as nothing but kids driving crazy fast and out of control—if C.J.'s partner hadn't been killed in a hit-and-run.

He would also love to know what C.J. was thinking now. Was she ready to admit that all this had to be about the kidnapping? Was she finally all in? He still couldn't be sure.

She came out shortly jingling a set of keys. Hank had left his keys in his car? What a trusting soul. It was a miracle the car hadn't been stolen. Not that he ever worried about that in Whitehorse. But this was Butte. He shook his head as he got out and followed her to the blue-and-white Olds.

Unlocking it, she opened the driver's-side door and stopped.

"What is it?" He glanced in expecting to see something awful. But the car looked spotless.

"His car never looks like this. Ever. He cleaned it out." She sounded shocked. And worried.

"So he cleaned his car. Because he was planning to go somewhere in it."

She looked skeptical. "Nowhere I can imagine that he would care."

Boone was disappointed. He'd hoped that they would find something in the car. If the man had cleaned it out, something rare, then he doubted there would be anything to find. "You want me to drive it?"

She shook her head. "I'll take it back to my place. You don't mind following me?"

He'd been following her since he got to town. "Not a problem."

She slid behind the wheel, but before she started the car, she reached up to touch what looked like a new small pine-scented car freshener hanging from the mirror. "This is so not Hank."

Boone went back to his pickup and caught up to her as they headed back to her house. In the distance, he could see the skeletal headframe over one of the old mine shafts, the dark structure silhouetted against the skyline. Another reminder he was in mining country.

Parking, he joined her, looking under the seat to see if Hank had missed anything. The smell of pine was overpowering from the small tree-shaped car freshener hanging from the mirror.

"What do you think he was covering up? A dead body smell?" he asked, only half joking. C.J. hadn't moved from the driver's seat, her hands still on the big steering wheel.

"I don't understand this change in him," she said as if more to herself. "He bought a cell phone, he canceled the landline at his office and had the power turned off. He packed his best clothes and cleaned out his car. It was almost as if…"

"As if he was leaving for good?"

She slowly swung her head around to look at him. There were tears in her eyes. "I need to get ready for the funeral."

"I'm going with you. Everyone knows that the killer always shows up at the funeral."

C.J. looked as if she wanted to put up a fight but didn't have it in her today after what had already happened.

"The problem is I didn't bring funeral attire."

She snorted. "This is Butte. I can promise you that most of the people there will be wearing street clothes because they're street people." She headed toward the house.

He waited until she went inside before he popped open the glove box. C.J. had already looked in it, but he'd noticed something that had caught his eye.

Like the rest of the car, it had been cleaned out, except for the book on the car. He pulled it out, noticing that it looked as if it had never been opened—except to stick two items into it. One was a boarding pass for a flight to Seattle. He looked at the date and saw that it was from last week—a few days before he was run down in the street.

The other was a train schedule. He flipped it over and recognized Hank's handwriting from the McGraw file the man had started. Hank had written dates and times on the back of the schedule—from Seattle to Whitehorse, Montana.

Chapter Twelve

The funeral was held in an old cemetery on the side of the mountain overlooking the city. C.J. used to come up here with Hank when he visited his long-deceased wife, Margaret. She'd asked him once why he never remarried.

When you have the best, it is hard to settle for anything else, he'd told her. *I didn't have her long, but I'm not complaining. I treasure every day we had together. She's all I need, alive or in my memories.*

The wind whipped through the tall dried grass that grew around the almost abandoned cemetery. But as she and Boone neared Margaret Knight's grave, the weeds had been neatly cleared away and there were recently added new silk flowers in the vase at the base of her headstone. Hank must have added them recently, she realized. Next to the grave site, C.J. saw the dirt peeking out from under a tarp and the dark hole beneath the casket.

C.J. had forgone a church service, deciding that

here on this mountainside was where Hank would have liked a few words said over him. He didn't go in for fanfare. In fact he preferred to fly under the radar.

Because he'd had something to hide? That was the question, wasn't it?

She pushed all such thoughts from her mind. She couldn't have been wrong about Hank. Just as all these people couldn't have been either, she told herself.

A crowd had already gathered and more were arriving, most of them walking up from town. A few had caught rides. Many were closer to Hank's age, but still the group appeared to be a cross-section of the city's population. All people whose lives had been touched by Hank Knight.

"Are all these people here for Hank?" Boone asked beside her.

She smiled through her tears and nodded. She saw the mourners through Boone's eyes, a straggly bunch of ne'er-do-wells who'd loved Hank. "These people are his family. They're all he had other than his late wife, Margaret." She frowned. "He once mentioned a sister. I got the impression she'd died when they were both fairly young. He'd once mentioned being an orphan." More and more she realized how little she'd really known about Hank.

As the pastor took his place, C.J. smiled at all the people who'd come to say goodbye to Hank. He would have been so touched by this, she thought as the pastor said a few words and several others chimed in before someone burst out in a gravelly rendition of "Amazing Grace."

C.J. felt as if a warm breeze had brushed past her cheek. Her throat closed with such emotion that she could no longer sing the words. Boone put his arm around her as the coffin was lowered into the ground and she leaned into him, accepting his strength. At least for a little while.

BOONE HAD BEEN to plenty of small-town funerals. Most everyone in town turned up. But he hadn't expected the kind of turnout that Hank Knight got on this cold December day in Butte, Montana. He was impressed and he could see that C.J. was touched by all the people who'd come to pay their respects to her partner. He could tell she was fighting to try to hold it together.

As he listened to the pastor talk, he studied those who were in attendance, wondering if Hank's killer was among them. He spotted one man who'd hung back some. He wore a black baseball cap and kept his head down. Every once in a while, he would sneak a look at C.J.

While the man's face was mostly in shadow, once when he looked up, Boone caught sight of what appeared to be a scar across his right cheek. The scar tissue caught in the sunlight, gleaming white for a moment before the man ducked his head.

Something about the man had caught his eye, but he had to admit there were a dozen others in the crowd who looked suspicious. Hank's clients were a rough-and-tumble bunch, no doubt about it. Anyone of them could have had some kind of grudge against him and done something about it.

But Boone's gaze kept coming back to the man in the black baseball cap. The moment the pastor finished, the man turned to leave. That's when Boone saw the way the man limped as he disappeared over the hill. Boone kept watching, hoping to see what vehicle the man was driving, but he didn't get a chance to see as the crowd suddenly surrounded C.J. to offer condolences.

She'd stood up well during the funeral, but as the mourners left, some singing hymns as they headed back into town, Boone could see how raw her grief was.

"I'll give you some time alone," he said and walked back toward his pickup. He hadn't gone far when he glanced back to see her, head bowed, body shuddering with sobs. He kept walking, moved by the love and respect Hank Knight had reaped.

When C.J. joined him at the pickup, her eyes were red, but she had that strong, determined set to her shoulders again.

"You must be ready for more food, knowing you," he said. "Where do you suggest we go where we can talk? I found something in Hank's car that I think you need to see."

Just as he suspected, getting back to business was exactly what C.J. needed. He drove to a Chinese food place on the way. It was early enough that the place was nearly empty.

After ordering, he took out the boarding pass and the train schedule. "I found both of these stuck in his vehicle book in a very clean glove box." He pushed the boarding pass across the table. She looked at it and then at him.

"I guess he really did fly to Seattle," she said, sounding sad.

"Who does he know there?"

"I have no idea. He's never mentioned anyone."

"And he's never been before?"

She shook her head, but he could see the wheels turning. "There were a couple times a year when he would take a few days off. I never asked where he went. I just assumed it was for a case. Most of the time he never left Butte. Or at least I thought he hadn't."

Boone nodded. "That's not all." He slid the train schedule across to her. "What do you make of this?"

C.J. studied it for a moment. "This doesn't mean he was planning to take a train," she finally said.

"Anyway, no passenger train comes through Butte. The only line is to the north up on the Hi-Line."

He flipped the schedule over. "Look what he had marked. The times for the train from Seattle to Whitehorse, Montana, and the date—day after tomorrow."

Her gaze shot up to his. "I don't understand."

"Your partner was going to meet that train."

She stared at him. "Talk about jumping to conclusions."

"Look at the evidence. He had packed, shut down his office and had this information in the glove box of his car. He flew to Seattle last week. Then he packed and cleaned his car. It seems pretty clear to me that he planned to drive north and meet the train when it came into Whitehorse."

"You're reading a lot into a train schedule and some scribbles."

She wasn't fooling him. He'd seen her expression when she'd recognized Hank's writing, the same way he had. "If you want to find his killer, then I suggest you come with me. Whoever gets off that train is the key."

"Go to Whitehorse?" She raised her eyes to his for a moment. "Let's say you're right. Even if we met this train, how would we know—"

"Whitehorse is just one quick stop for the train. Our depot isn't even manned. Only a few people ever get off there. It shouldn't be that hard to figure out who Hank was meeting. This is about my sister and her kidnapping. Come on, C.J. You aren't going to keep arguing that it's not, are you?"

She met his gaze. He had that urge to gather her up in his arms, kiss her senseless and carry her away. "Whitehorse," she repeated.

He could see she looked scared. "You coming with me?"

BY THE TIME Boone dropped her off at her house to pack for their trip the next day, it was already getting dark. This was why she hated winter hours. Living in Butte, she'd gotten used to the snow and cold. As Hank used to say, *It invigorates a person and makes them really appreciate spring.*

Back in her house, she pulled out her suitcase, but was too antsy to start packing. She made herself a cup of tea and went to sit by the front window. She loved her view of the city below. It had sold her on this house. The view and the small deck off the front. During the warm months, she spent hours sitting out there watching the lights come on. This house had filled her with a contentment—a peace—that she feared she would never feel again.

Hank's death, the revelations he'd left behind, Boone... She thought of the handsome cowboy. Did he really think he was helping her? Just being around him left her feeling…discontent. Certainly no peace. He made her want something she'd told herself she wasn't ready for, didn't need, didn't want.

C.J. shook her head at the memory of being on the street when she'd been so sure he was going to kiss her. He'd been staring at her lips and she'd felt… What had she felt? A tingling in her core. An ache. She'd felt desire.

She groaned. "And now you're really going with him all the way to Whitehorse, Montana, wherever that is? Have you lost your mind?" Her words echoed in the quiet house. She picked up her tea cup and took a sip.

At moments like this she felt the grief over Hank's death more profoundly. She swallowed back a sob as she thought of his funeral and all the people who had shown up. They'd loved him. She'd loved him. He'd saved her when she was a child. Her mother had been struggling just to keep her head above water. Hank had taken up the slack. He'd given C.J. purpose.

So was it possible that he could have been dirty? How else did she explain all that money in those stocks and bonds he'd left her?

Her head ached. None of this made any sense and hadn't since Hank was killed. Exhaustion pulled at her. She'd known the funeral would be hard. She just hadn't realized how hard. But seeing all the people who loved Hank had helped. Just the thought of them brought tears to her eyes again. They couldn't all have been wrong about Hank.

Her mind reeled at the thought of Hank keeping whatever had been going on with him from her. She felt betrayed, adrift. Had he planned to leave town for good and not even mention it to her? Why would he do that?

Because it had something to do with Jesse Rose and her kidnapping. Which meant that Hank either thought it was too dangerous to tell her or… Or he didn't want her to know what he was involved in because he was up to his neck in something illegal.

Either way, there was no more denying it. This was about Jesse Rose and the McGraw kidnapping case. Hank had been to Seattle, and right before he was killed. She had no idea what that might have to do with the second trip he was apparently planning. Seattle was to the west, while Whitehorse, Montana, was up on the Hi-Line in the middle of the state. What did the two places have to do with each other, except for the fact that the McGraw ranch was outside of Whitehorse?

Nor did she have any idea of who he might be planning to meet on the train from Seattle. The same person he'd visited in Seattle in the days before he was killed?

As if all of this wasn't troubling enough, Hank

had a whole bunch of money that he'd left to her and she had no idea where it had come from.

Maybe more upsetting than him not telling her about it was the fact that he'd cleaned his car, packed his best clothing and shut down his office as if…as if he wasn't coming back.

Tears filled her eyes. Had he been running away? Then why the train schedule? Was he meeting someone on that train coming from Seattle to Whitehorse? Someone he planned to abscond with?

A shock rattled through her at the thought. Had she known Hank Knight at all?

But that was just it. She *had* known him. He had been a good man and there was a good explanation for all of this. She just had to find it. That meant going to Whitehorse and meeting that train from Seattle—with Boone.

"You should get some rest," Boone had said when he'd dropped her off. "I'll pick you up in the morning. I hope you'll go with me."

"I—"

"Sleep on it," he had said quickly. And for a moment, he'd gotten that look in his eyes.

She shivered now at the memory and touched her upper lip with the tip of her tongue. She almost wished the man would just kiss her and get it over with. That made her smile.

Wiping at her tears, she turned off the light and

started out of the dark living room in the direction of her bedroom. She'd only taken a few steps when she heard the noise and stopped. Her gaze shot to the window. She hadn't realized that the wind had come up. It now whipped the branches of the tress outside.

That must be what she'd heard. One of the branches scraping against the side of the house. Only the noise she'd heard… It had sounded like someone trying to pry open a window. Like a lock breaking?

She reminded herself that last night she'd thought she'd seen a man standing out in her yard and it had turned out to be a shadow and nothing more.

A dark shadow swept past the glass. Her breath caught in her throat as her heart began to pound. Someone was out there trying to get in.

She rushed to the table where she'd dropped her purse when she'd come into the house. As she heard another noise down the hallway in her bedroom, much like the first, she managed to fumble her cell phone from her purse. Her fingers brushed her gun as a louder noise came from the back of the house. It had been one of the old cantankerous windows being forced open.

Her heart pounding, she pulled out the pistol, snapped off the safety and laid it on the table as she turned her attention to her phone. She hit 911, all the time estimating how long it would take for the police to get there. Too long. That's if they even came. Once they knew it was her calling, they'd just think she was being a hysterical woman again. Just like she'd been when she'd told them that Hank's hit-and-run had been murder.

BOONE HAD DRIVEN all the way back to his motel but he hadn't pulled in. Something kept nagging at him. He hadn't wanted to leave C.J. alone tonight. After that near so-called accident earlier, he feared she wasn't safe.

Of course, she'd argued that she was fine. She would lock her doors. She had a gun. She could take care of herself.

But still, he didn't like it. He kept thinking about the man he'd seen at the funeral in the black baseball cap. He'd meant to ask C.J. about him. Something still nagged at him about the man. Was it possible he'd been driving the car earlier that had almost run them down?

Reminding himself how exhausted C.J. had looked, he told himself that he could ask her about it tomorrow. She probably wouldn't even know who the man was. Then again, she seemed to know everyone in Butte.

Swearing, he swung the pickup around and went back, knowing it would nag at him until he asked her. Also, it wouldn't hurt to check on her as long as she didn't think that was what he was doing. He told himself that if all the lights were out, he wouldn't bother her. But if she wasn't asleep yet...

As he neared the small house overlooking the city, he saw that the lights were all out. He couldn't help being disappointed. He wasn't good at leaving things undone and for some reason, this seemed too important to wait.

He started to turn around since her house was at the end of dead-end street, a deep gully on one side and an empty lot on the other. Walkerville was even older than uptown Butte since this is where much of the original mining had begun. The houses were small and old, but the view was incredible, he noticed as he swung into her driveway to turn around.

The pickup's headlights caught movement at the back of the house.

IN THE DARK living room, C.J. put down the phone as she heard a loud crash at the back of the house—and picked up the gun. She moved slowly down the hallway toward the back of the house and her bedroom, the gun clutched in both hands in firing position.

She spent hours at the shooting range—but she'd never had to use her weapon as a PI. She hoped she wouldn't tonight.

The cold wind that had chilled her at the funeral earlier had picked up even more. She could feel a stiff breeze winding down the hallway from where someone had opened the window.

Stopping to listen, she heard nothing but the wind and the occasional groan of the old house. She knew most of those groans by heart. What she feared she would hear was the creak of old floorboards as someone moved across them headed her way.

The house was dark, except for the cloud-shrouded moonlight that filtered in through the sheers at the windows. Shadows played across the hallway.

As she neared the bedroom where the noise had come from she could make out the glittered remains of her shattered lamp on the floor. What she couldn't see was her intruder. Snaking her hand around the edge of the doorway, she felt for the light switch. She'd just found it when the curtain at the window suddenly snapped as it billowed out on a gust of wind, making her jump.

She found the light switch again and readied herself. Her intruder had either left. Or he was waiting in the pitch-black corners of her bedroom to jump out at her.

BOONE CUT HIS lights and engine and was out of the pickup in a heartbeat. He ran toward the back of the house, realizing belatedly that he should have grabbed something he could use for a weapon.

The dark shadow he'd seen was gone. He was

telling himself that the person had taken off when he'd been caught in the beams of the pickup's lights. Then he saw the open window and the large over-turned flowerpot someone had used to step on to climb into the house.

His mind whirled. Had C.J. had time to go to bed? He looked around, not sure what was beyond this open window. The person he'd seen could have dropped off into the ravine next to the house and could be long gone. Or he could have gone into the house and was now inside. He could have C.J.

Boone pulled out his phone and quickly keyed in her number. He waited, listening to the wind and his heart, for the phone to ring. And prayed she hadn't turned hers off.

C.J. JUMPED AS her phone rang in the other room. She glanced back down the hallway, distracted for a split second.

At a sound in the bedroom, she turned back, but too late. A large dark figure came busting out of the bedroom. She raised the gun, got off a wild shot, heard a groan. But then she was hit by the man's large, solid body as he crashed into her. He knocked the breath out of her, slamming her back against the wall before she hit the floor hard, gasping for breath.

Her phone was still ringing as she rolled to her stomach, the weapon still clutched in her hand. All her training took over as her intruder pounded toward the front door. "Stop!" she cried, leveling the laser beam on the man's back.

He was fumbling at the door lock.

C.J. pushed herself up to her knees and tried to hold the gun steady. "Stop!" It happened in slow motion, but only took a few seconds. She raised her weapon, the laser jittering in the middle of his back as her mind raced. Pull the trigger? Shoot him in the back? Or let him leave? She'd seen that he was limping. Had she hit him with the first shot she'd fired?

"Don't make me shoot you!" Her voice broke.

He got the door unlocked, flung it open and stumbled out into the night. As her phone stopped ringing, she leaned back against the wall, still holding the gun, her heart thundering in her chest.

BOONE HEARD THE phone ring inside the house just moments before he heard the gunshot and the pounding of feet headed toward the front of the house. He raced in that direction in time to see a large dark figure come running out of the house, leap the porch railing and disappear over the side of the yard and into the ravine. As he did, Boone saw that the man was limping badly.

"C.J.!" he yelled as he ran up onto the porch. "C.J., it's me, Boone. Are you all right?"

"Boone." Her voice sounded distant and weak.

He rushed into the open doorway and fumbled for the light switch. An overhead fixture blinked on, blinding him for a moment. He saw her cell phone on the table next to her open purse.

"I'm all right."

He turned on the hall light and following her voice, he found her sitting at the end of it, the gun resting between her legs. Bright droplets on the wood floor caught his eye. Blood. He rushed down the hall to drop to his knees next to her. "Were you hit?"

She shook her head. "I fired the only shot. I think I caught him in the leg. He was limping."

"Did you get a look at him?" he asked as he pulled out his phone to call the police.

"Don't do that."

He looked up at her in surprise. "But your neighbors…"

"They've heard gunshots before. They won't call it in."

"But—"

"If we hope to meet that train in Whitehorse, we don't want to get involved with the cops, not now. It wouldn't do any good anyway. Nothing was taken. I didn't get a good look at him. And I don't have the best relationship with the cops in this town right now." There was a pleading in her gaze. "I'll just clean up the blood." She pushed herself to her feet.

Boone wanted to argue but he remembered what

the detective had said about PIs. Apparently she was right about their relationship. It wasn't one-sided.

He rose with her. He could tell that she was still shocked and off balance. He knew she wasn't thinking clearly. But he couldn't disagree about what would happen if they called the cops. A shooting would mean a lot of explaining. She was right. They had to meet that train if they hoped to find out who had killed her partner and why—and what it might have to do with Jesse Rose and her kidnapping all those years ago.

But what had this been about tonight?

"I'll take care of the window," he said as he moved to the bedroom. The lock had been broken. "I could pick up a new lock at the hardware store in the morning to fix this."

"I don't think he'll be back."

"So you think it was a robbery gone wrong?"

She shrugged, avoiding his gaze. "What else?"

"How about something to do with Hank's death?"

C.J. finally looked at him. "Why would you say that?"

"Because I saw a man at the funeral. He had a scar on his cheek, wore a dark baseball cap pulled low. Ring any bells? He was limping—like the man who just ran out of here."

She frowned. "He doesn't sound familiar. You said he was limping at the funeral?"

"Yes. He kept his face hidden beneath the brim of his baseball cap except when he was looking at you. He seemed to have a lot of interest in you. And unless I'm mistaken, the man you just chased out of here was wearing a dark baseball cap."

SHE'D SHOT HIM! Cecil couldn't believe it. He drove back to his motel room, parked where he couldn't be seen from the office and limped inside. His leg hurt like hell and it was still bleeding. The blood had soaked into his jean pant leg.

He pulled out the motel room key, opened the door and slipped inside. In the bathroom, he pulled down his jeans and looked at his leg. It wasn't as bad as he'd thought it was going to be.

The bullet appeared to have cut a narrow trench through the skin. At least the slug hadn't hit bone. Nor was it still in there. That was something, since that leg had already been injured years ago. He still had the scar, a constant reminder of how badly things had gone that night.

Opening the shopping bag he'd picked up at the convenience mart, he pulled out the alcohol bottle, opened it and, gritting his teeth, stepped into the bathtub and poured the icy liquid over his wound.

He had to hold on to the sink to keep from passing out from the pain. What hurt worst was that he'd failed tonight. He pulled the length of cord from his pocket. It should have been around C.J. West's neck.

His cell phone rang. He checked caller ID. His ex-wife. He'd been trying to get back together with her, because he still loved her. Also he needed her more than she could know. He let it ring another time, before he took her call. As he watched his blood stain the white porcelain of the cheap motel room tub, he said cheerfully, "Tilly, I'm so glad you called. I was just thinking about you."

Chapter Thirteen

Boone rubbed his neck and stretched as best he could as he drove.

"You should have taken the bed last night," C.J. said.

"The recliner was fine." He'd had enough trouble convincing her to come to his motel last night. It was that or the two of them staying in her house. He hadn't liked the idea that the man might be the same one who'd tried to run her down and then broken into her house. He wasn't taking the chance that the man might come back.

"At least at my motel, he won't know where you are."

"I can get my own room."

"Could you possibly just let me take care of you for one night? Two brushes with death in one day? Haven't you been through enough today?" She'd given him a look he couldn't read. "Come on, you need sleep. Right now, it appears that the only thing keeping you on your feet is pure stubbornness."

She'd finally relented. But when they'd gotten to the motel, she'd wanted to argue about who was going to take the bed.

"*You're* taking the bed. You want the bathroom first? Then get in there." When she'd come back out he'd gone right into the bathroom after, giving her a warning look not to argue with him.

Exhaustion had taken her down. When he came out of the bathroom, she was lying on the end of the bed as if she'd been sitting there and had just keeled over for a moment to rest.

Shaking his head, he'd picked her up and carried her around to the side of the bed. He'd never met such a mule-headed woman. She reminded him of... He'd chuckled. She reminded him of himself.

She'd barely stirred but he'd hushed her up as he took off her shoes and tucked her into the bed. Then he'd stood there for a long moment watching her sleep before he'd headed for the recliner.

Not that he'd been able to fall asleep. He kept thinking about C.J. Her loyalty to Hank. Her determination to find his killer at all costs. Her sweet, vulnerable look when she was sleeping. It made him smile.

C.J. West was a complicated young woman who intrigued him more than he wanted to admit.

HIS LEG HURT like hell. Cecil hadn't gotten any sleep. The first thing he'd had to do was put a new bandage on his gunshot wound. Now standing in the bathroom naked, he braced himself for the pain. Pouring more of the rubbing alcohol on the wound, he let out a cry and clutched at the sink.

At least the wound had stopped bleeding, he thought as he covered it with gauze and then a bandage before pulling on his jeans. He hadn't thought to bring more clothing. He hadn't thought out a lot of things, he realized. So many mistakes. And now he couldn't go into a store the way he looked. No, it didn't matter how he was dressed. He needed to finish this.

At the thought of how badly that had gone last night, he wanted to scream. If Boone hadn't come back… Not that he could blame him.

He'd rushed it, just wanting to get it over with instead of waiting until he knew she was asleep. Once inside the house, he'd had a chance to finish it. He'd knocked her down. How much harder would it have been to take the gun away from her, choke the life out of her or use the gun on her?

His first plan had been to wait until she was in bed asleep and then sneak in and put a pillow over her head. He knew he couldn't do it looking at her. But he'd gotten impatient and couldn't wait for her to fall asleep. He had a piece of cord in his pocket. He'd thought that he could get behind her and strangle her as long as he didn't have to see her face.

But things had gone badly. He'd panicked. Isn't that why he hadn't killed her in the hallway last night? It had been so close and personal. Nothing like running someone down in a car.

But he'd even failed at that. His life had been one failure after another. Now if he didn't want to spend the rest of his life in prison...

With a groan, he limped out of the motel bathroom. He had to go back to C.J. West's house. If she wasn't there, maybe he could wait inside for her. Wait and surprise both her and Boone when they came back.

But when he'd gone by her house he'd seen one of her neighbors out in his yard. He'd parked and gotten out, limping over to him.

"I was looking for the woman who lives in that house," Cecil said, and realized he might be able to pass for a delivery boy even at his age. "She placed an order. I was trying to deliver it."

"Must be some mistake," the man said, eyeing him. "I saw her leave this morning with a suitcase. I got the impression she wouldn't be back for a while. Left with some man. What did you do to your leg?"

"Old war injury," he lied.

"Sorry you came all this way. Is it anything I can take off your hands?"

"No, I don't think so, but thanks for the informa-tion." He limped to his vehicle and climbed painfully back in. She'd left with a *suitcase*?

He quickly called Boone McGraw's motel only to be told that he'd checked out. Swearing, he tried his ex-wife's number, telling himself that Tilly prob-ably wouldn't know anything if she answered. Since she'd gone back to work, often she was vacuuming the McGraws' big new house and didn't even hear her phone.

She picked up on the second ring. "Hi." She sounded a little breathless. He pictured her with a duster in her hand standing in one of the many bed-rooms. She'd been dark-haired when he'd married her all those years go. Now over fifty, she'd gone to a platinum blonde as if thinking it made her look younger.

"Hi," he said. "Busy?"

"These cowboys," she said with a sigh. Tilly usu-ally could find something to complain about. He wondered what she'd found during the years that they had been divorced.

"Well, at least you have less to clean with Boone gone," he said.

"Ha! I just heard not only is he on his way back, but he's bringing some…" she lowered her voice "…woman. I have to get a room ready for her."

"No kidding?" So they were headed back to

Whitehorse, back to the ranch. He swore silently. He'd never be able to get to her at the McGraw Ranch. Even though security wasn't as bad out there as it had been following the kidnapping, it would still be impossible to break in without getting caught.

But then again, he had Tilly there, didn't he? No one would suspect anything if she brought her ex— and soon-to-be husband again—out to the ranch where she worked to see the new house.

"How did the job interview go?" she asked now, reminding him of the reason he'd given her for leaving town for a few days.

"I'll tell you all about it when I see you. I'm about to head home. I'd like to take you out to dinner when I get back."

"A date?" He could hear the pleasure in her voice and should have felt guilty for all the lies.

"Why not? You're still my Tilly girl, aren't you?"

C.J. LOOKED OUT at the passing landscape of towering mountains and deep green pines. Boone had told her it was a six-hour drive. She'd wanted to take her own car, but she knew he was right. It made sense to go with him since they were going to the same place, he knew the way and someone was after her. So it was safer being with him, at least according to him.

She hated this feeling of vulnerability and Boone McGraw only made it worse. Being around him left her feeling off balance. Before all this, she'd felt she had control of her life. She'd felt safe knowing what she would be doing the next day and the day after that. She had a plan.

Hank's death had changed all that. She'd lost her biggest supporter. She'd lost her friend and the man who'd filled in all these years as her father. Boone showing up had turned an already confusing time into... Just the freshly showered male scent of him made it hard to think. And she needed desperately to figure this all out. It's what she did for a living. She solved mysteries. She helped people, just as Hank had taught her.

But right now she felt as if she couldn't even help herself. Too many of the pieces were missing and her grief over Hank's death had her too close to tears most of the time.

She rubbed a hand over her face and told herself to quit whining. She was still strong, still determined. She'd gotten through her mother's death. But only because Hank had been there for her. Now she felt... alone. And yet not alone, she thought as she looked over at Boone.

"Thanks for last night."

He shot her a glance. "No problem." His smile warmed an already unbearably handsome face.

She felt her heart do a little tap dance against her ribs and was glad when he turned back to his driving. "I keep going over it in my head. There's no reason anyone would want to harm me."

"You were Hank's partner. Whatever he knew, the killer must assume you knew it, as well. Or realized that you were looking for the truth."

But she knew nothing. The fact that Hank hadn't told her what was going on with him hurt heart-deep. Her head ached from trying to understand what had been going on with him in the days before his death. So many secrets. Not just the stocks and bonds, but Seattle. And maybe Whitehorse as well?

"So tell me about your family," she said and turned to look at Boone, desperately needing to get her mind on something else.

BOONE GLANCED AT her in surprise. "You mean more than what you've already read about my family? I doubt there is much to tell." He knew she'd researched the kidnapping. As she'd said that first night, she didn't leave things to chance.

"I did some research, but it's not the same. You have two brothers you grew up with, Cull and Ledger. So what are they like?"

He could see that she seriously wanted to know. He suspected it was only to keep her mind off the long trip—and what she'd been through the past week—but he was happy to oblige.

"Cull's the oldest, the bossiest." He laughed. "He's great. You'll like him. He's a lot like you, actually," he said and glanced over at her. They'd left Butte behind and now traveled through the mountain pass toward the state capital.

"How so?" she asked suspiciously.

"Stubborn to a fault. Determined to a fault. Independent to a fault. But he's changed since he fell in love." He saw her turn more toward him as if he'd piqued her interest. "He and Nikki St. James, the crime writer, are engaged. She came up to the ranch to do research for a book and her digging around set some things off."

"I heard it also almost got her killed. I suspect I'm going to like her."

He chuckled and nodded. "I suspect you will."

"And Ledger?"

Boone sighed. "Ledger. He fell in love in high school with a girl named Abby. They broke up when he was in college, some misunderstanding perpetrated by her mother, and she married someone else. A bad idea on her part since her husband was abusive."

"Wade Pierce."

"Yep." He grinned. "You probably know all this."

"No, please continue."

He studied the road ahead for a moment, thinking. "But Ledger, also a bit stubborn and determined, hung in there, determined to save her."

"Sounds like someone I know," C.J. joked. "Did he?"

"He did. They're finally together again. This time I don't think anything will tear them apart."

"So you're the last single brother."

Out of the corner of his eye, he could see that she was smiling. But he wasn't about to take the bait. "Actually, my brother Tough Crandall is still single."

"Right, the one who doesn't want to be a McGraw. Oakley McGraw, the missing twin."

"Yep. Talk about stubborn. I suspect he will always be Tough Crandall. He's made it very clear that he doesn't need the McGraws or want what comes with us—lots of unwanted publicity."

"I guess I can understand that. You don't think he will come around eventually?"

"My dad does. Dad never gave up looking for the twins, never gave up believing they were still alive, just never gave up. Of course, my dad is one of those men who looks at a half-full glass and thinks it is three-quarters full. You'll meet him."

"One of those," she said with a shake of her head and a smile.

"He's never given up on finding the twins, even when we wished he would," Boone said. "For years, the kidnapping has defined us all."

"Probably why you can't get a date," she joked.

He smiled over at her. "I had a date the other night at the steakhouse."

She shook her head. "You call that a date?"

"I would have if I'd gotten up the nerve to kiss you."

C.J laughed and met his gaze. "So why didn't you?"

"I kept thinking about that gun in your purse. I didn't want to feel the barrel poking me in the ribs."

"You're smarter than you look." She turned to glance out the windshield as they passed Helena and began the climb again up another mountain pass. "Strange, the paths our lives take. Not always easy. Was it horrible growing up with the kidnapping hanging over you?"

"Not all the time. My brothers and I love horses so we spent a lot of time on the back of one. We stayed away from the house during the bad times, especially when the anniversary of the kidnapping rolled around. There was always something in the newspaper—thanks to our Dad. That's why I have to help find Jesse Rose if she is still alive. Maybe then Dad can just enjoy his family."

"You're lucky to have such a large family, and with your brothers getting married…"

"Yes, and it's growing. One of the reasons Dad wanted the new house to be so large. He wants plenty of room there for all the family. You'll see."

She shot him a look.

"We're staying out at the ranch." He held up a hand before she could argue. "I'm not letting you out of my sight until this is over. I know you're very capable of taking care of yourself, but if I'm right, the reason someone wants you dead is because of my family tragedy. So let me do this."

She'd opened her mouth to speak, but closed it for a moment. "Fine. Is your stepmother still behind bars?"

He laughed. "Last I heard, thank goodness. Patty, yes. Still locked up so it's safe." He shook his head at thought of her. "I told you that she didn't just try to kill my father by poisoning for months with arsenic—we believe she did the same thing to my mother twenty-five years ago. When Patty wants something… And she wanted my father—until she got him."

"Do you think she was the kidnapper's accomplice?"

"I certainly wouldn't put it past her. But if so, her plan backfired. She didn't get my father—at least not then. She went away for nine years. The only reason she came back when she did was she needed a home for her and her baby."

"Sounds like she had another reason for returning to your ranch and just used the baby to get what she wanted."

He smiled over at her. "It certainly worked. My father raised Kitten all those years only to have Patty send the girl off to some relative. Kitten was a lot like her mother so while it was hard on my father to see her go…"

C.J. nodded. "A lot of drama?"

"Since she was little."

"So what was it like growing up on a horse ranch?" she asked as she made herself comfortable in the passenger seat.

"It was an amazing childhood, actually." He began to tell her about learning to ride at an early age, of horseback rides up into the Little Rockies, of swimming in the creek and racing their horses back to the corral. "Cull usually won, but there was this one time…"

Boone glanced over to see that C.J. had fallen asleep. He smiled and looked to the road ahead. He couldn't shake the feeling that his life had changed in some way he'd never planned. It unsettled him. But soon they would be on the ranch. And once Jesse Rose was found… Well, things would get back to normal. Right, normal—as if that was ever going to happen.

Chapter Fourteen

C.J. felt a hand on her shoulder and sat up quickly, suddenly awake. She couldn't believe she'd fallen asleep. But she'd had trouble sleeping since Hank's death. Last night was the best sleep she'd had in days, but she was still exhausted.

"Where are we?" she asked, looking around. The earlier mountains covered in tall pines had given way to prairie.

"Great Falls. I thought you might be hungry."

Her stomach rumbled in answer, making him smile. She really did like his smile. She wished he smiled more. He was far too serious most of the time, she thought and realized she could say the same about herself.

"Fast food? Or take our chances at that café over there?"

"Given everything that has happened to me recently, I'm up for taking a chance on the café."

"Brave woman. I like that about you," he said

as he climbed out of the pickup with her right behind him.

She joined him at the table he'd selected by the window after going to the restroom to freshen up. The café smelled of coffee and bacon and what might have been chili cooking in the back and another scent that made her think of the meals her mother used to fix. Something with burger and macaroni.

As she slid into the booth, she realized she liked the feel of the place. It reminded her of the cafés she loved in Butte. Sun shone in through the window, warming their table, and she felt herself relax for the first time in days.

She had to admit that part of it was her companion. Boone was easy to be around. He made her laugh and he seemed to get her. She thought of some of the men she'd dated and groaned inwardly. Not that she'd thought a cowboy could ever turn her head. Was that what Boone had done?

"Your family knows we're coming?" she asked as she picked up the menu in front of her to chase away that last thought.

"Dad does. Not sure if he told my brothers. We discussed keeping it quiet. Just in case."

She looked up from the menu. "Just in case Hank's killer doesn't know about any of this?"

Boone shrugged. "I can only hope. Based on a train schedule and some of his doodling, I think

Hank planned to meet that train tomorrow. But I don't think his killer has this information. Otherwise, why not just meet the train and stop whatever it is from happening? Why try to run you down and later break into your house?"

She shook her head. She had no idea. None of it made sense. She thought of the thumb drive. More and more she hated keeping it from him. She started to say something when the waitress interrupted.

"Know what you'd like?" the waitress asked suddenly at their table.

"What is your soup today?" C.J. asked.

"Homemade chili with a side of corn bread."

"That's what I thought. I'll have that."

"I'll have the same," Boone said and handed back his menu.

"Anything other than water to drink?"

They ordered colas and were silent as the waitress left. She felt the thumb drive in her pocket, but the moment had passed. She had to wait and see who got off that train. The mystery of who might be arriving on that train had her anxious as well as worried. But she thought that Boone was right, that Hank had planned to meet whoever was coming in from Seattle tomorrow.

"So tell me about growing up in Butte," Boone said. She knew he was asking only to distract her. But he listened as if with interest as she told him

about her mother's job in Hank's building at a sec-
ondhand store, how back then there were lots of fun
junk shops in town and lots of customers.

"But your favorite part was working with Hank,"
he said when she finished.

She smiled. "On the weekends I was like any
other kid. I rode my bike with friends, played in
mud puddles, snooped around in abandoned houses
and made up stories. I always thought I'd write books
one day."

"Really? Then you and Nikki really will hit it off."

Their chili and corn bread arrived and they dove
in, both seeming to enjoy the meal as well as the
quiet. They had the café to themselves since it wasn't
noon yet. Other than the occasional clatter of dishes
or pots and pans in the back, the only sounds were
the murmurs of enjoyment from them. The chili was
good. So was the corn bread, especially with fresh
butter and honey.

C.J. finally pushed back her empty plate and bowl.

"How are you feeling?" Boone asked, having finished his.

"Good." The realization surprised her. For the
first time in days, she felt as if she might live through
this. Which made her laugh. A killer was after her
and yet… She smiled over at Boone. "I'm good. Want
me to drive for a while?"

THE PAIN IN his leg was worse today. Cecil hoped it hadn't gotten infected. As he drove toward White-horse, he tried to think about what to do next.

Tilly hadn't been able to give him much information other than Boone McGraw was returning to the ranch with a woman. That much he'd figured out on his own. The question was why?

Had they found out the truth and were now going to Travers with it? He told himself that they couldn't have. Not yet. But once they found Jesse Rose, once they started putting the pieces together like Hank Knight must have...

He thought about the night of the kidnapping. So many years ago. They'd all changed so much. Tilly had been twenty-five and pretty as a picture. Patty, the nanny, hadn't been much of a looker back then, just a mousy-looking girl. Nor had the older cook been anything to look at.

Things had definitely changed after the kidnapping. The first Mrs. McGraw, Marianne, was now in the loony bin, crazier than a mad hare. Travers Mc-Graw had gone downhill. Now sixty, he'd recently had a heart attack and almost died. Of course, he blamed the nanny who he'd foolishly made his second wife for trying to poison him to death. Patty had most certainly outgrown that mousy look she'd had when she was the nanny.

He shook his head. He could understand why Tilly had liked working out there. She loved minding other people's business and that ranch was a hotbed of gossip.

I'm invisible in that house, she'd once told him. *I can be standing in the same room with my duster and it's as if they don't even see me. They just go on as if I'm not there.*

Smiling in spite of the pain, he recalled how he had loved her stories about what he thought of as the rich and famous. At least in Whitehorse, Montana. Tilly was as much part of that house back then as those walls that he'd often hoped couldn't talk.

It had been on one of his visits to his wife at the old McGraw house that he'd met Harold Cline. Harold had been dating the ranch cook, a stout middle-aged woman named Frieda. He'd wondered at the time about that arrangement since Harold wasn't a bad-looking guy. So when Harold had asked him if he'd like to get a beer, he'd accepted. Actually anyone who was buying back then would get a yes from him.

At a local Whitehorse bar, the two of them had sat in a corner and shot the breeze. After the weather and how work sucked, they talked about what was going on at the ranch.

Like Tilly, Harold's girlfriend had filled Harold in on all the comings and goings. The big topic had been the first Mrs. McGraw, who'd had a set of twins six months before and was now acting strangely. Tilly had been worried about her as well, saying she didn't seem to have any interest in the twins.

"Frieda's worried that Marianne might do something to the babies," Harold had whispered after four beers. "Terrible thing. Apparently, she didn't want any more kids and now she doesn't want anything to do with the twins. Frieda's worried she might hurt them. One night the nanny caught her in the nursery holding a pillow like she was going to smother them."

He'd been shocked to hear this, not that Tilly hadn't expressed concern about Marianne McGraw, saying the woman seemed confused a lot of the time.

I sure hope nothing bad happens to them. Cute little things. Sure would be a shame, Harold had said and bought another round of beer.

Cecil couldn't remember when Harold had mentioned getting the babies out of there before something terrible happened to them.

The plan had seemed so reasonable back then. Harold knew some families who would take care of them until their mother got better. They'd been saving those babies.

But even later when it became clear that they were going to kidnap the McGraw twins for money, Cecil hadn't put up a fight. In fact, by then he'd been out of work for months, Tilly was threatening to leave him and he would have done just about anything to get his hands on some money.

Two hundred thousand dollars? he'd whispered in shock when Harold had told him how much ransom they could get.

It isn't like McGraw doesn't have it. All those fancy horses, that big house, and look at what he pays your wife and my girlfriend, Harold had said.

Actually, Tilly had gotten paid well and been well taken care of out at the ranch. That had been part of the problem. She'd had it so good out there that she'd been thinking she could do better than Cecil, but he'd kept his mouth shut and gone along with the plan. If Tilly had left him like she'd been threatening then he would need the money.

It had crossed his mind that Harold might try to cheat him out of his share. But the man couldn't pull off the kidnapping without him so he'd told himself not to worry.

The night of the kidnapping, Tilly had called to say she was sick and asked if he could bring her some cold medicine. Her timing couldn't have been more perfect.

He'd driven within a mile of the ranch near the Little Rockies. Harold had followed him in his rig. They'd hidden it in the pines, then Cecil had driven on out to the ranch with Harold hunkered down in the back. Tilly had left the side door open for him.

While he'd gone upstairs to take the cold medicine to Tilly, Harold had climbed out and hidden in the pool house. He'd already found a ladder he could use to get to the second floor window of the twins' room.

He'd given his wife a double dose to make sure Tilly was out cold. While he was waiting for her to sleep, he'd noticed a bottle of codeine cough syrup sitting there. Tilly had said Marianne McGraw had given it to her from an older prescription she'd had. Later, Marianne wouldn't remember doing that.

Once Tilly had been asleep along with everyone else in the house, he'd walked down the hall and pretended to leave. Instead, he'd ducked into the twins' room and given each of them some of the codeine cough syrup, hoping he didn't overdo it. Careful not to leave any prints on the bottle other than his wife's and the babies' mother's, he'd left it in the twins' room.

Then he'd waited in a guest room down the hall until it was time. Better to be caught there then in the twins' room. Finally it had been time. He'd checked the hallway. Empty. Not a sound in the house. He'd made his way down to the twins' room, still shocked that he was actually doing this. Both babies had been sleeping soundly.

Cecil had opened the window as Harold climbed up. He'd wrapped up the babies in their blankets with their favorite toys just in case the infants woke up.

He'd handed them out and Harold had put them in a burlap bag and then descended the ladder.

He'd been thinking how they'd pulled it off when he'd heard a loud crack and had looked out the window to see that one of the ladder rungs had broken under the big man's weight. He'd thought then that it was all over, but somehow Harold had managed to hold on—and not drop the babies.

Then he'd gotten the hell out of there, scared out of his wits. Back at his vehicle, he'd driven back to where he'd left Harold's vehicle but it had already been gone. They'd planned not to meet until the ransom was paid. Cecil never saw him again, let alone his half of the ransom money.

He'd been so shaken that night that he'd just taken off, driving too fast, not even knowing where he'd been going. He'd lost control of his car miles from Whitehorse and spent the next week in the hospital in a coma.

It wasn't until recently that he'd learned what had happened to Harold and the ransom money. It had given him little satisfaction to find out from the news that Harold was dead and the money found with him in his shallow grave.

The only good news was that no one knew who had helped Harold from inside the house. But then Tilly had told him about Hank Knight, convinced that the PI knew not only what had happened to Jesse Rose, but who the second kidnapper had been.

Now he looked at the highway ahead, telling himself he might still be able to get away with it. As long as Boone and that female private investigator didn't find Jesse Rose, he should be in the clear. But as he drove, he couldn't help but worry that they knew something he didn't. He could be driving back to Whitehorse—right into a trap.

Chapter Fifteen

C.J. found herself smiling as she drove. She listened to Boone's breathing as he slept. He looked so content, not anxious like he did when he was awake. She felt she'd gotten to glimpse something few people had seen. A peaceful Boone McGraw.

The highway took them from Great Falls up to the Hi-Line and across the top part of the state. They were just outside of Whitehorse when Boone stirred.

He sat up, looking surprised that he'd let himself fall asleep. All semblances of peace and serenity left his handsome face as he glanced out the window and saw where they were.

"You need to turn up here at the next road," he said. "You okay driving? If you pull over I can—"

"I'm fine. Nice nap?"

He looked embarrassed. "I didn't realize that I'd fallen sleep, let alone that I was conked out that long. Thanks for driving. I guess I was more tired than I thought."

She merely smiled and seeing the turnoff ahead, slowed. "We aren't going into town?"

"I thought we'd go straight to the ranch."

"I'd feel better staying at a motel—"

"Not a chance. Since I'm not letting you out of my sight, you'll be much safer on the ranch than in a motel in town." He glanced in his side mirror as if, like her, he wondered if whoever was after her might be somewhere behind them.

"I don't think we've been followed," she said. "I've been watching."

He leveled his gaze at her as she turned onto the dirt road. "I keep forgetting you do this for a living."

She said nothing for a half mile. "What will your family think, me showing up on their doorstep with my suitcase in hand?"

"I'll carry your suitcase," he said.

"You know what I mean."

"They'll think…" For a moment he seemed to consider what they would think. He swore under his breath. "My brothers will give you a hard time. They'll think you and I have more than a professional relationship."

"But you'll make it clear that's all it is, right?"

"Of course. You need to turn up here. See that sign reading No Buffalo? Hang a right there." He glanced straight ahead. "This was all too complicated to explain on the phone. But don't worry. The new house is large with numerous guest rooms. While I've been gone, a designer has been putting the finishing touches on it. My father will be delighted to have you."

"So you all live in the main house?"

"I have a place on the ranch, a cabin, where I usually stay. But until this is over, I'll be sleeping at the house in a room next to yours."

If he thought that made her feel safe, he was sadly mistaken.

Ahead, the house came into view. She stared, a little awestruck. It was beautiful. Boone had mentioned it was new. She'd read about the explosion and fire that had burned down the original house.

She felt anxious about meeting his family and braced herself. So much felt like it was on the line right now. She thought about the thumb drive in her pocket, feeling guilty for keeping it from Boone, from his family.

But only until tomorrow, she told herself. Whatever happened at the train, she would show it to Boone.

As THEY PULLED into the ranch yard, Cull and Ledger were coming up from the barn. Boone saw their interest in who was driving his pickup and swore again under his breath. The last think he needed was them giving him a hard time about C.J.

Also he'd hoped to talk to his father first. Even better would be to tell everyone at the same time to save repeating himself. But he could tell by the inquisitive looks on his brothers' faces that they were more than curious about the woman behind the wheel of his pickup.

"Looks like you're going to get to meet my brothers right away," he said as she handed him the keys. He opened his door, hopped out and called a hello to them. Not that his brothers noticed him. They were staring at C.J.

Cull lifted a brow as he and Ledger joined them. "Hired yourself a chauffeur?"

"This is C.J. West. She's a private investigator."

Cull shook her hand. "I'm his older smarter, more handsome brother, Cull."

"And this is Ledger," Boone said, wishing his brothers could behave for once.

As C.J. shook his younger brother's hand, Cull said, "I hope you've brought good news."

Just then their father came out on the porch.

"Can we take this inside? I'll tell you everything I know," Boone said with a sigh. "But C.J. and I will be staying at least overnight."

"I'll help you with your bags," Ledger said. "Go on in. I know Dad is anxious to hear what you found out."

"So am I," Cull said.

Boone led C.J. up to the house, introduced her to his father and the three of them entered the new house.

The old one had been huge and quite opulent. This one was more practical. It had a nice big eat-in kitchen, a large dining room and living room, a master suite for their father and a ranch office. The other bedrooms were divided between two wings off the north and south ends of the house on the same level to provide privacy for anyone staying in them.

His father had gotten it into his head that his sons and their wives would be staying over a lot so he would be able to spend even more time with his future grandchildren.

The interior designer his father had hired had been given only one requirement. *Marianne loves sunny colors*, Travers had told her. *We need this house to feel like sunshine.*

Boone had to admit, as he stepped into the house, the designer had done her job well. She'd been finishing when he'd left for Butte. The house looked inviting and at the same time homey. It never had with Patty in command. He was anxious to ask his father what had been going on while he'd been gone, with Patty's upcoming trial, her threat to write a tell-all book and a rumor that more arrests would be made in his father's poisoning case.

"Do you mind if I freshen up while you bring your

father up to speed?" C.J. asked as Ledger brought in their bags. He could tell she wanted to give him and his father and brothers time alone and he appreciated that.

"Take the last room on the south wing," his father told her. "And please let us know if there is anything you need or want. Boone—"

"You can put my bag in the room next to hers," Boone said, making his brothers as well as his father lift a brow.

C.J. didn't seem to notice as Ledger steered her toward one of the bedroom wings, leaving the three of them alone.

"Why don't we step into the office?" his father suggested.

They'd barely gotten seated when Ledger joined them. Like the old office, there was a rock fireplace with a blaze going in it and comfortable chairs around it along with a large oak desk.

Boone told them what had happened since he'd last seen them.

"Hank Knight is dead?" Cull said. "And you say C.J. was his partner in the investigation business?"

"She's a licensed private investigator and worked with him. But they were much closer than that. Hank helped her single mother raise her. C.J. and Hank were very close. It's one reason she is determined to find his killer."

Cull was shaking his head.

"What does the C.J. stand for?" Ledger asked.

"Calamity Jane. She said her father was a huge fan of Westerns."

"And he's deceased?"

Boone nodded. "Died when she was two."

"So you think this person who's made attempts on her life—and yours—is somehow connected to the kidnapping and Jesse Rose?" his father asked.

"It seems that way. All we know is that Hank Knight didn't share any of it with C.J., something highly unusual, according to her. And he'd flown to Seattle, also something unusual since he apparently hated to fly. He appeared to be planning another trip before he was killed. That, I believe, was to White-horse. We think he planned to meet the train from Seattle tomorrow in Whitehorse at 2:45 p.m."

"Who is coming in on the train?" Travers asked.

Boone shook his head. "We have no idea. But we plan to be there."

"What if no one gets off from Seattle?" Cull asked.

"Then my theory is wrong and then I don't know." Boone raked a hand through his thick dark hair, his Stetson resting on his knee. "It's possible that none of this has to do with Jesse Rose."

"Then what?" Ledger asked.

He shrugged. "But someone wants to keep C.J.

from finding out the truth about her partner's murder. If his inquiries about Jesse Rose and the kidnapping are what got him killed…"

"I want to meet the train with you tomorrow," his father said.

"I'm not sure that's a good idea. I think it would be better if C.J. and I go alone. Whoever is getting off that train is expecting to meet Hank Knight. If there's a crowd," he said, looking pointedly at his brothers, "it might scare them away."

"You're hoping Jesse Rose gets off the train," Cull said. "Would you recognize her?"

"I think so."

"And if it is someone else, someone…dangerous?" Travers asked.

"I can handle myself, and don't forget—I will have a card-carrying, gun-toting private investigator with me."

C.J. PUT HER suitcase on a bench in the last room at the end of the hall where Ledger had led her. The room was lovely, bright and airy with a large sliding glass door that looked out on the mountainside beyond. She could see where it appeared a swimming pool was going in to the right. To the left were corrals and several large barns.

Opening the doors, she stepped out on the patio.

Three horses watched her from a nearby corral. She smiled and walked over to them.

She was stroking one of the horse's neck when she heard someone come up behind her. She didn't turn around, didn't need to. She knew it was Boone. That connection that had been growing between them felt stronger than ever.

"You like horses." He sounded surprised. "We could go for a ride. It's a beautiful afternoon and tomorrow it's supposed to snow. We should take advantage of this weather."

She could tell that he wanted to go for a ride. "Why not?"

"I'll saddle us up a couple of horses. Come on." She followed him into the cool of the barn and watched while he expertly saddled the horses. "I gave you a very gentle one."

"I appreciate that." She smiled as he offered her a foot up. She placed her shoe in his cupped hands and let him lift her. Swinging her leg over, she settled in the saddle. It had been a while since she'd ridden a horse, but it felt good. She took the reins and watched Boone. He looked completely at home in the saddle.

They rode out into the afternoon sunlight. It was so much warmer here than it had been in Butte. She breathed in the fresh air as they rode slowly across a pasture.

"Those are the Little Rockies," Boone said, pointing to the dark line of mountains in the distance. "The story goes that Lewis and Clark originally thought they were the Rocky Mountains. When they realized their mistake, they renamed them the Little Rockies."

C.J. saw some cabins back in a stand of trees. "Is that where you usually stay?"

He nodded. "But see that land on the hillside over there? That's my section. Someday I'm going to build a house on it with a view of the mountains."

"When you get married. Is that what your brothers are doing, building on their land?" She pointed to a spot where some land had been excavated.

"That's my brother Cull's. He and Nikki will start their house in the spring. Ledger and Abby will be building about a half mile farther from there. We all wanted to be close—but not too close."

"So you'll always stay on the ranch," she said, not looking at him.

"That's what I've always planned."

She looked over at him because of something she heard in his tone. "Unless?"

"Unless I fall in love with someone who doesn't want this life."

"You'd go where she wanted?" It surprised her that he thought a woman could get this cowboy off the ranch.

"For the right woman, I would."

They rode in silence as the sun slid farther to the west before they turned back.

BACK AT THE RANCH, Cull came out to say that their father wanted to talk to C.J.

"You go ahead," Boone told her. "I'll take care of the horses and join you in a minute."

"You told them that I don't know anything, right?" she said to him.

He nodded. "But you knew Hank Knight."

"I thought I did."

"It's all right," Boone said. "My father understands."

She followed Cull back into the house. Travers McGraw was waiting for her in his office. He rose to his feet when she entered and she saw that he wasn't alone.

"This is Nikki St. James, the true crime writer who is doing the book on the kidnapping."

C.J. shook hands with Nikki, recalling what Boone had told her about the woman. She'd thought at the time that she would probably like the writer. The woman was pretty with long dark hair and wide blue eyes.

Travers asked C.J. to tell them more about her and her relationship with Hank. She told them about growing up in Butte and the impact Hank had on her life.

"I wish I could tell you more," C.J. said after she'd told them what she knew about Hank's inquiry about Jesse Rose and the kidnapping.

"You said Hank always shared his other cases?" Nikki asked. "Had he ever been involved with adoptions?"

"No."

"Do you know if he knew a woman named Pearl Cavanaugh? She was a member of the Whitehorse Sewing Circle."

She shook her head. She'd thought she'd known everything about Hank. That he could have lived a secret life, or worse, that he was involved in the McGraw kidnapping, seemed inconceivable.

Boone came into the room and took a seat. He gave her a reassuring smile.

"How old are you?" Cull asked. He'd been sitting quietly in a corner, listening. She had almost forgotten he was there. Unlike Boone. Her nerve endings had tingled as he'd walked into the room. She'd never been more aware of a man.

"Twenty-eight," she said, wondering why he was asking.

"So you would have been three at the time of the kidnapping," Boone said and looked at his father. "She would have been too young to know if Hank was involved back then."

"He couldn't have been involved in the kidnapping," C.J. argued. "You didn't know him. He wouldn't…" She felt her eyes burn with tears. "He spent his life *helping* people. He didn't steal babies from their beds."

"I wasn't implying that," Nikki said quickly. "One of the kidnappers who was involved was told that the babies weren't safe. We think that's what gave Harold Cline the idea of kidnapping them. It could also be the reason that someone in that house helped him. At least one of them could have thought they were saving the twins."

C.J. felt her stomach roil. If Hank had thought he was saving the babies… "If he was involved, why would he call your lawyer and ask questions about Jesse Rose and the stuffed toy horse that was taken with her?"

She saw Travers and Boone share a look before Nikki said, "He could have been worried about this new information that was released regarding the kidnapping. If Jesse Rose still had the stuffed toy horse and she heard about it or her adoptive parents did…"

"Wouldn't they have contacted you?" C.J. asked.

"The parents might be afraid of losing their daughter, getting into trouble with the law… There are a lot of reasons they wouldn't want to come forward, especially if they knew who she was when they received her," Travers said.

"As for Jesse Rose, she might not even know that

she was adopted," Nikki said. "Even if she saw the digitally enhanced photos in the newspaper, she might not think anything of it."

"But if she had a toy horse with a pink ribbon tied around its neck, she might start asking questions," Boone said. "If the horse gave the six-month-old baby comfort, the adoptive parents might have kept it."

"Or they might not have known that the stuffed toy horse came from the McGraw house," Nikki said. "They could have thought it was a gift from whoever had taken the baby to save her."

"Once it hit the news, though…" Boone looked to C.J.

She felt sick at the thought of all this. That Hank might have been involved twenty-five years ago… She revolted at the idea. Not the Hank she thought she'd known. She reminded herself that he'd kept whatever was going on from her. Because of shame? Or to protect her because he knew it was dangerous?

That thought gave her a little hope. While it looked bad, there was still the chance that Hank was innocent. After all, he was a PI. He could be working for someone who was neck deep in this and was looking for a way out.

"I guess we'll find out tomorrow, depending on who gets off that train at the Whitehorse depot," Boone said. "Until then all we can do is speculate.

You must have seen the digitally enhanced photos in the newspaper and on television. Or looked them up on the internet. Did you ever see anyone who resembled Jesse Rose with Hank?"

"No," she said with a shake of her head and suppressed a shudder at the thought of the thumb drive with the young woman's photo on it. She hated lying and promised herself that after tomorrow, she would show it to Boone and his family. She hated keeping secrets from him. But she also couldn't betray Hank.

If Jesse Rose got off that train, she'd recognize her.

Chapter Sixteen

C.J. said she'd like to lie down for a while. Boone took that opportunity to go into town before dinner. "Don't worry, I'll be back in plenty of time," he told his father.

He drove straight to the sheriff's department and asked to see Patty, his former nanny and stepmother. When she'd been his nanny, she'd had straight brown hair, appeared shy and reserved.

When she'd returned to the ranch nine years later with a baby in her arms, she'd changed in more ways than her bleached hair color, from everything that Boone had heard. All he knew was that she'd certainly conned his father. Travers had married her to help her raise the baby, father unknown. Patty had been hell on wheels for those years as his stepmother. She'd made all their lives miserable.

Boone was just glad to have her out of their lives.

The dispatcher started to explain the visiting hours schedule when Sheriff McCall Crawford came out.

"I need to see Patty," he said, "and I'm not going to be able to make visiting hours for a while."

"Probably just as well since she posted bail and will be released later this evening," the sheriff said.

"What? How?"

McCall shook her head. "She came up with the bail and got a judge to grant it. It's out of my hands."

Boone pulled off his Stetson to rake a hand through his hair. "Then I really need to talk to her before she's released."

The sheriff hesitated for only a moment. "Just keep it short, okay?"

He nodded and let her lead him to the visiting room. He'd barely sat down when Patty slid into the seat on the other side of the glass. She smiled at him before picking up the phone.

The smile was enough to set him off, but he reined it in. He came here hoping for information. Ticking her off wouldn't get him anything except maybe a little satisfaction.

"You're looking good," he said into the phone.

She smiled at that. "You McGraws are such charming liars. Heard you'd been out of town. Go somewhere fun?"

"Butte. Went to see a PI who had information on the kidnapping."

"Really?" Her expression hadn't changed. "So you got it all solved, do you?"

"Not quite. Where is my mother's diary?"

She shook her head. *"Diary?"*

"I know you have it."

"You're wrong. Everyone thinks I'm responsible for whatever was going on in that house twenty-five years ago. Well, I wasn't the only drama."

"We know about Frieda and her love affair that set off the kidnapping."

Patty smiled. "That was just the tip of the iceberg. Tilly ever confess anything to you?"

Tilly? Their housekeeper?

"I believe Tilly had taken cold medicine the night of the kidnapping and was knocked out and had to be awakened."

Patty just smiled.

"Are you trying to tell me it isn't true?" When she said nothing, he lost his cool. "Dammit, Patty, I know you poisoned my mother twenty-five years ago and then did the same thing with my father over the past year. I know you, remember? I saw how you treat people."

She leaned forward and lowered her voice. "Boone, I'm a bitch, but I'm not a killer. Nor did I poison anyone."

He studied her, surprised that a part of him believed her. Was it possible she might be telling the truth?

"Then who was poisoning my father?"

"Anyone with access to that house. Your former ranch manager, Blake Ryan. Your family attorney, Jim Waters." She shrugged. "They ate at the house all the time."

"What was their motive?"

She looked away for a moment. "Maybe they thought they'd get me and the ranch if Travers was gone."

"Where would they get an idea like that, I wonder?"

Patty swung back around. "Not from me."

"Frieda is dead, thanks to you. Or are you going to tell me that you had nothing to do with that, either?"

"I didn't."

He narrowed his gaze at her. "You had a lot to lose if she talked."

"But not as much as the person who helped with the kidnapping. Yes, I kept Frieda in line with what I knew about her boyfriend. Like I said, I was a bitch but I had nothing to do with killing her."

"Sounds like you're innocent of everything."

"I didn't say that. I've made my share of mistakes. My biggest regret is your father. Believe it or not, I loved him. But I always felt like I was living in your mother's shadow—because I was. He never loved me the way he did her and I knew it."

With Patty in a talkative mood, he had to ask. "Who is Kitten's father?"

She laughed. "Who knows? That's not true. It was nobody. A one-night stand. A handsome guy at a bar when I was feeling vulnerable."

"Not Jim or Blake or my father?"

She shook her head.

"Jim and Blake both think they're her father."

Patty shrugged.

"Again, I wonder where they got that idea?"

She smiled. "Like I said, I'm not innocent of everything." Sighing, she looked him in the eye. "What do you want from me, Boone? I'm about to blow this place and I doubt we'll be talking again for a while, if ever."

"The truth would be nice."

"I guess you'll have to wait for my tell-all book," she said with a sad smile and replaced her phone as a deputy came into the room.

C.J. SAT AROUND the big table in the dining room and listened to stories about the boys growing up. It felt good to laugh. She especially liked the stories about Boone.

"He was five when he tried to ride one of the calves," Cull was saying. "He hung on all right. Straight across the pasture. We thought we'd probably never see him again. He was hootin' and hollerin'." They all laughed.

"Came back looking like he'd been dragged

through the mud, as I recall," Ledger said. "Told everyone he'd ridden a bull."

C.J. loved the sound of their laughter. It was clear that they all loved each other. She felt the warmth and the camaraderie. And for a while, she forgot what she was doing there with them. Forgot about the thumb drive she kept in her pocket. Forgot that Hank was dead. And worse, that someone might be getting off the train tomorrow who would forever change the way she felt about the man she'd loved as a father.

By the time she'd gone to bed, all she wanted was the oblivion of sleep. She'd thought her thoughts would keep her awake. But the moment her head touched the pillow she was out. In her dreams, though, she kept seeing Jesse Rose's face. The woman was trying to tell her something, something about Hank, but C.J. couldn't hear her because of the noise from the train.

BOONE STAYED UP late talking with his father and brothers. It felt good to be back at the ranch. He'd needed that horseback ride earlier. It was the only place he felt at home.

He couldn't help thinking about C.J.—and what he'd told her on the horseback ride. Would he really leave the ranch for a woman? Not just any woman, but her?

Unable to sleep he went outside. It was a clear,

cold night but he needed the fresh air. He loved it here, loved the dark purple of the Little Rockies on the horizon, and the prairie where thousands of buffalo once roamed.

He thought of Butte and C.J. Would she leave it for a man? For him?

Shaking his head, he couldn't believe the path his thoughts had taken. He hadn't even kissed the woman. But at dinner tonight, he also couldn't keep his eyes off her. She was so beautiful. He thought of her with that ragtag bunch of half-homeless people at the funeral. She'd called them her and Hank's family. He doubted he'd ever met anyone with such a big heart.

Or anyone more stubborn.

"I know that look."

He turned to see Cull come outside.

"Something bothering you?"

Boone let out a laugh. "Seriously? I'm terrified that I'm wrong about this whole thing. Who knows if there will even be someone on the train tomorrow and now I've got Dad's hopes up and—"

"What's really got you out here wandering around in the dark?" Cull asked, cutting him off.

"I just told you."

His brother shook his head. "Like I said, I know that look. You think I didn't wander around in the dark after meeting Nikki?" Cull let out a laugh.

"I used to go out in the barn and talk to myself. I thought I was losing my mind. How could I fall for a damned true crime writer—one who turned our house upside down for a story?"

Boone chuckled. "You've got it all wrong."

"Just keep telling yourself that. A private investigator from *Butte*? Wondering how you got to this point in your life, aren't you?" He held up his hands. "Don't bother lying. I saw you out here and thought I could dispense some sage advice. Take it from me. I've been there. So just go for it. Seriously. Anyone with eyes can see how crazy you are about her. Stop kidding yourself. You've fallen."

Boone shook his head. "You should get some sleep, big brother. You're talking out your—"

"Yep, just keep telling yourself that," Cull said as he laughed and headed in the direction of his cabin.

Boone watched him go. "Just go for it? Right. So much for sage advice, big brother."

STOPPING JUST OUTSIDE the sheriff's department mid-morning, Patricia "Patty" Owen McGraw breathed in the fresh air and looked toward the deep blue sky overhead. A Chinook had come through and melted all the snow, but she'd heard a couple of deputies talking about a white Christmas. A storm was supposed to blow in by this afternoon.

She'd completely forgotten about Christmas. Her

only thought had been freedom. And now here she was. Free. At least for a while.

"Are you all right?" asked the deep male voice next to her in a tone that told her he didn't really care. Probably never had.

"I am now," she said without looking at the former McGraw ranch manager. Blake Ryan wasn't one of her favorite people right now. Hell, no one was.

"You realize it's temporary," he said. "Only until your trial. If you take off, you lose—"

"I know what I lose," she snapped and took another deep breath. Having Blake pick her up from jail had been a mistake. He hadn't wanted to do it. She'd had to almost beg and when that failed, she'd had to resort to blackmail. It seemed no one wanted to get on the wrong side of Travers McGraw.

You betrayed Travers when you slept with his nanny twenty-five years ago—not to mention his wife much more recently, she'd snapped on the phone earlier. *He knows about us, so come pick me up. I need a ride and you need me to keep at least some of the things about you out of my book.*

"This money they advanced you on this tell-all book," Blake said now as he opened the car door.

"What about it?" She couldn't help the irritation in her voice. It was none of his business. She owed him nothing.

"Do you have to give it back if you don't write the book?"

"Why wouldn't I write it?"

He shot her a look and cleared his voice. "Patricia, you can't tell *everything*." She suspected Travers had set up some sort of retirement plan for the ranch manager and still contributed to it. Everyone had their reasons for distancing themselves from her, but they would all pay when the book came out. Or when this went to trial.

She glanced out the side window. "I told the publisher it was a tell-all book that dished the dirt. All the dirt. You wouldn't want me to have lied, would you?" She smiled to herself as she felt his gaze on her before he turned back to his driving.

"It wouldn't be the first time you lied," he finally said.

She burst out laughing as she turned back to him. "I wondered if you'd have the guts to call me on it. And you did. What is it you're afraid of, Blake? How about I write that you were an amazing lover?"

"I don't think that's funny."

"I wasn't trying to be funny. I meant what I said, I'm telling it all. Anyway," she said with a shake of her head as bitterness rose like bile in her stomach. "What do I have to lose? Do I have to mention that I asked for your help and you couldn't be bothered?"

"You know the position I'm in."

"Unlike the one I'm in?"

"Patricia, give me a break. I don't have the kind of money you need to get out of this."

"But I sure found out who my friends and lovers were, didn't I?" She bit at her lower lip as silence filled the truck. "You're in this just as deep as I am."

"Where do you want to go?" he finally asked. "You want a drink? Something to eat? We could swing by Joe's In-n-Out for a quick lunch."

His offer was like a knife to her heart. He didn't want to be seen with her, hoped to get rid of her as quickly as possible. She studied him for a moment, glad she didn't have a knife because it would be in Blake's chest right now. Why did she always fall in love with weak men?

"Just drop me at the Great Northern Hotel." Had she thought earlier that he would have wanted to take her to his place? Would she have gone if he had asked her?

He drove around the block and pulled up at the entrance to the GN, as it was called locally. As she opened her door to get out, he said, "I wish you wouldn't do this."

She glanced back at him. "Spend a night in a motel room alone?"

"You know what I mean."

She laughed and forced a smile. "You mean what I tell during my trial? Or the book? I'm going to give you a whole chapter, Blake," she said and slammed the door. She didn't look back as she fought the burn of tears.

"HOW IN HADES did Patty make bail?" Boone demanded as he stormed into his father's office. "I just heard. Tell me you didn't—"

"I didn't."

"Did you know?"

His father shook his head. He pushed away the papers in front of him and sat back in his chair. "She must have sold the book she's been threatening to write about the kidnapping. Her tell-all book. She tried to get me to buy her off. I don't care what she writes."

Boone swore. "Well, if anyone knows the truth about what happened that night, I'm betting it was Patty." He frowned. "But that kind of truth won't set her free."

"Maybe she knows more than she has ever told about someone else being in the house that night," Travers said.

"Is that what you're hoping?" he asked.

"Truthfully? I just want Jesse Rose found. As far as the other kidnapper…"

"You don't want justice?"

"Justice." Travers chuckled. "There can never be

justice. Too much was lost." He got a glazed look in his eyes.

Boone studied his boots for a moment. "How *is* Mom?"

"Better. She wants to see Oakley."

He looked up in surprise. "You told her about Tough Crandall?"

"He's her son."

"Are you sure about that?" He ground his teeth at the thought of the arrogant cowboy who'd paid them a visit to set them straight. Tough Crandall had outed the man pretending to be Oakley.

But Tough had refused to take a DNA test to prove that he was the lost twin. In fact, Tough wanted nothing to do with the McGraws—any of them.

"Has Tough agreed to see Mother?"

"Not yet, but he will."

Boone shook his head. His father had lived in a fantasy world for twenty-five years, first believing the twins were alive and would come home one day. And now he thought that cowboy who'd known for years that he was the missing twin—and kept it from his own grieving birth father—would find it in his heart to visit his birth mother?

"Dad—"

"Boone, he just needs time."

He told himself that he didn't want to argue the point with his father. He didn't have time anyway.

He and C.J. had to meet the train. He'd had trouble getting to sleep last night and had been anxious all morning. Cull's little talk with him hadn't helped.

Now he tried to concentrate on what had to be done. He just hoped that whoever was on that train knew something about Jesse Rose's whereabouts. That was if she was still alive. That thought was the fear that had dogged him since his father had asked him to talk to PI Hank Knight.

Oakley had been found—kind of—not that it was the happy reunion his father had hoped for. But that didn't mean that Jesse Rose would be found. Twenty-five years was a long time. Anything could have happened.

C.J. FOUGHT TO still her nerves as they drove into Whitehorse. The afternoon wind sent a tumbleweed cartwheeling across the road in front of them as they reached the outskirts of town.

"This is Whitehorse? And you made fun of Butte?" C.J. joked as she took in the small Western town.

"Easy," he said and grinned. "You're in the true heart of Montana."

She scoffed good-naturedly at that as he pulled up to a small building that had Whitehorse printed on the side. She recalled that he'd said it was unmanned.

Tickets were bought online. There was only one car parked next to the depot but no sign of anyone.

Across the tracks was apparently the main drag. She saw a hotel called the Great Northern, several bars, a restaurant and a hardware store. Like a lot of towns, Whitehorse had sprung up beside the railroad as tracks were laid across the state.

Looking down the tracks, though, she saw nothing in the distance. They got out into the waning winter sunlight. The air smelled of an impending snowstorm. C.J. shivered although it wasn't that cold as they went to stand on the platform in front of the depot. The train was due to arrive soon, but they were the only ones waiting.

She could tell that Boone was as anxious and worried as she was. Looking down the tracks for the light of the locomotive, she tried to keep her emotions in check. If they were right, Hank had been planning to meet this train.

"What if a dozen people get off the train?" C.J. asked, merely needing to make conversation because she knew exactly what Jesse Rose looked like.

"Not likely,'" he said with a laugh. "This will probably surprise you, but like I told you, not many people get off here."

"That is a surprise," she said.

He smiled over at her. "This area of Montana would grow on you. If you gave it a chance."

She met his gaze. "You think?" She thought about what he'd said the day before. That he'd leave for the right woman. But no woman who'd seen him on his ranch would ever take him from what he loved. No woman who loved him, anyway.

"Ever thought about a change of scenery?"

"Whatever are you suggesting, Mr. McGraw?"

He shrugged as if embarrassed.

What *had* he been suggesting? Whatever it was, he seemed to wish he hadn't brought it up. "You know, if you ever got out this way in the future."

Little chance of that, she thought as snowflakes began to fall. In the distance, she thought she heard the sound of a train.

BOONE COULDN'T BELIEVE what he'd just said to her. What *had* he been suggesting? Whatever it was, it wasn't like him. Like he could take Cull's advice. Like he ever would. And yet he'd realized this morning that no matter who got off that train today, C.J. would be leaving.

He'd take her back to Butte and that would be it. That thought had made him ache. C.J. had gotten to him, no doubt about that. She was funny and smart. He loved the tough exterior she put up. But he could see the vulnerability just below the surface. It made him want to protect her and he knew the kind of trouble that could get him into. Look at his brothers.

But now, as he waited for the train, he couldn't help looking at her as if memorizing everything about her. Her cheeks were flushed from the cold. Her eyes were bright. He watched her stick out her tongue to catch a snowflake as if not even realizing she'd done it.

"We could wait inside," he suggested, seeing her shiver.

Hugging herself, she shook her head. "I think I heard the train."

He could guess what she was hoping. That whoever was on this train would know who might have wanted Hank Knight dead. C.J. wouldn't rest until she found her partner's killer.

He hoped he was around when that happened. C.J. might just find out that she did need someone. Even him. While he loved her independence, he'd learned it was okay to lean on family occasionally. He got the feeling that it had only been her and Hank against the world for too long, and now with her partner gone...

As much as he fought with his brothers and knocked heads with his father, Boone was damned glad he had them in his life. He couldn't imagine how alone C.J. must feel. He felt another stab of that need to protect her.

Not that there was any reaching out to her. She'd rebuffed any attempt to offer comfort. She was determined to go it alone and had only grudgingly put up with him because she had no choice. But she had let him put his arm around her at the funeral. She'd even leaned into him. For a few minutes.

Snowflakes whirled around them. C.J. had her face turned up to the snow, her eyes closed. He saw her shiver again and couldn't help himself. He stepped to her and pulled her close.

She opened her beautiful brown eyes and looked at him. He felt his heart bump against his ribs. He wanted this woman. The thought terrified him. And yet he wrapped her tighter in his arms and drew her into him as the snow spun around them.

Chapter Seventeen

C.J. looked up into Boone's blue eyes as he pulled her against him. She forgot the falling snow, the cold and the worry and pain that had seeped into her bones over the past week. In his arms, she felt warm and safe.

All her instincts told her to pull away, but she didn't move.

Her gaze locked with his and she felt her heart quicken. Slowly, he bent his head until his lips were only a breath away from her own. She couldn't breathe. Didn't dare. She thought she would die if he didn't kiss her.

His lips brushed over hers. She let out a sigh of relief and joy and pleasure. He pulled her tighter against him, taking her mouth with his own. She melted into him and the kiss, heart pounding, desire sparking along her nerve endings like a string of lit dynamite.

The sound of the train whistle on the edge of town

made them both jump, bringing them back to reality with a thud. As they stepped apart, C.J. braced herself as the light on the front of the locomotive came into view.

The train puffed into town through the falling, whirling snow. Boone stood next to her as the noisy train slowed and finally came to a stop after numerous cars had gone past. Boone hadn't said a word after the kiss. Nor had she. But she did wonder if he regretted it.

She touched the tip of her tongue to her upper lip and smiled to herself. Not that it would ever happen again, she was sure. Neither of them was ready for... for whatever that had been.

A door opened on one of the coach cars. A conductor put out a yellow footstool and then began to help a passenger off. C.J. held her breath but let it out on a frosty puff as an elderly woman was helped off, followed by an elderly man. They walked toward their vehicle parked beside the depot where they'd apparently left it before their trip.

C.J. felt her heart drop. She shot Boone a look as the locomotive engine started up and the conductor picked up the stool and stepped back on to close the door as the train began to move again.

"Boone?"

The train began to slowly pull away. She wanted

to scream. She wanted Boone to take her in his arms again. Tears blurred her eyes.

"It's all right," he said, touching her arm. "They still have to unload the sleeping car."

She blinked. The train hadn't left. She heard it grind to a stop again after going only a short way. This time a door opened on a sleeping compartment car next to the platform. Another conductor stepped off with a stool and reached back in to bring out a suitcase. He set the case on the cold concrete and then reached back in again—this time to help a young woman off the train.

C.J.'s hand went to her mouth as the dark-haired young woman from Hank's thumb drive stepped off and looked in their direction.

Boone made a sound, as if equally startled by the intensity of the woman's green eyes. She was beautiful, slender and graceful-looking in a way that C.J. feared she would never be. Her heart felt as if it might burst. She knew she was looking at Jesse Rose McGraw— and all that it meant.

Oh, Hank, what were you involved in?

She looked over at Boone, gripped by a wave of guilt for withholding the thumb drive. She could see him struggling, as if asking himself if this woman could be the sister he hadn't laid eyes on since she was six months old.

C.J. felt her chest constrict as she touched his

shoulder. He looked over at her and she nodded. The train pulled out and was gone as quickly as it had come, leaving the three of them standing in the falling snow.

It was Jesse Rose McGraw all grown up. C.J. stared at the woman through the falling snow, her heart hammering with both relief and fear. She couldn't keep kidding herself. Hank had been involved in all this up to his ears.

"Excuse me," Boone said as they approached the young woman. "Were you expecting to meet Hank Knight here?"

Tears filled the young woman's eyes as she looked past them for a moment, before settling her gaze on C.J. "Hank…" Her voice broke. "He's gone, isn't he?"

C.J. nodded, not sure how the woman had heard about Hank's death, but glad they weren't going to have to give her the news. "I'm so sorry."

"You must be Calamity Jane," the young woman said through her tears as she stepped to C.J. and threw her arms around her. "Uncle Hank told me so much about you."

Uncle Hank? C.J. shot a surprised look over Jesse Rose's shoulder at Boone. He looked as shocked as she felt.

"But I'm surprised *you're* here," the young woman said as she pulled back to look at C.J. "He said it would either be him or…" Her gaze went to Boone. "Or someone from the McGraw family."

C.J. saw her wipe at her tears as she turned to Boone.

Her face lit as she smiled. "You must be one of my brothers?"

"Boone McGraw." He sounded dumbstruck but at the same time overjoyed. "And you're…"

The young woman held out her hand. "Jesse Rose Sanderson."

"Jesse Rose?" he repeated in obvious astonishment as he took her gloved hand in his.

She smiled sadly. "Uncle Hank told me that he tried to talk my mother into changing my name, but I guess when she whispered the name to me the first time she held me, my eyes lit up. She didn't have the heart to change it."

Boone shook his head. "So you know… We definitely need to talk, but we don't have to do it out here in the snowstorm." He ushered them toward the large SUV that he and C.J. had brought into town from the ranch.

C.J. climbed in the back so Jesse Rose could be up front with her brother. As she did, Jesse Rose reached back to clasp her hand.

"Calamity Jane," the young woman said with a laugh. "You're exactly as Uncle Hank described you. But I know you prefer C.J. Sorry. I've always loved your name and wanted to meet the girl who'd stolen my uncle's heart." Jesse Rose's hand was warm in hers. C.J. wondered if she could feel her trembling. Hank had told Jesse Rose all about her?

"I was so hoping Uncle Hank would be meeting the train, but he'd warned me that he might not be able to make it. Was he very sick at the end?"

C.J. shook her head, completely confused. *Sick?*

"I hope he didn't suffer."

"No," she said quickly. Everyone who'd seen the accident said he'd been killed instantly. "He didn't suffer." She felt as if she'd fallen down a rabbit hole.

"Good," Jesse Rose said. "He looked fine when he was out in Seattle but my mother said cancer can do that. She said then that he wouldn't be with us long."

Cancer? C.J. couldn't believe what she was hearing. Was it true? And yet as she sat there staring at the falling snow outside, she knew it was. Hank's sudden decision to retire. It had been so unlike him. He'd loved what he did. She'd tried to talk him out of it but he'd made all kinds of excuses. She'd finally stopped pushing him, seeing that he'd been determined. And yet, she'd also seen how sad he'd been about the decision. Now it made sense.

But why hadn't he told her? She tried to remember if she'd ever seen him looking sick and realized there had been a couple of times when she'd stopped by his office and caught him unaware. She'd just thought he was tired, that the job had taken a toll on him. She'd never dreamed... Cancer.

It explained so much. Why he'd be so set on retiring and closing down his office. Why he'd flown to Seattle without telling her and why he'd warned Jesse Rose than he might not be meeting the train. That one of the McGraw brothers would meet the train. Clearly, he'd planned on going, otherwise he would have let someone at the McGraw ranch know. But then he hadn't planned on getting run down in the street, had he?

Jesse Rose let go of C.J.'s hand as Boone climbed behind the wheel. "I'm just so glad that Uncle Hank told me about my family out here."

"So how long have you known?" Boone asked as he started the SUV. C.J. could tell that he was hoping this wouldn't be another case of a child who didn't want to know her McGraw family like Tough Crandall.

But C.J. suspected the woman wouldn't be here right now if she didn't want to get to know her birth family.

"Known I was adopted? Or known that I had more family?" Jesse Rose asked.

Boone shifted into Reverse. "Both."

"I found out I was adopted when I was seventeen. I was looking for my birth certificate…" She shrugged. "I found it and it said I was born to my parents, but I also found a letter from a woman named Pearl Cavanaugh. Did you know her?"

"I knew who she was," Boone said.

"I only learned recently, though, about the circumstances of my adoption. Uncle Hank told me—over the protests of my mother. He said it was time I met my birth family."

"What about your father?" C.J. had to ask.

"My father died when I was twelve. My mother was apparently the only one who knew that I'd been kidnapped, but according to Uncle Hank, she had wanted a child so much, she would have kidnapped one herself if she hadn't gotten me."

Boone glanced in the rearview mirror at C.J. as he drove through the underpass and down a block before pulling in front of the Whitehorse Café. He couldn't imagine what was going through her head right now. His was still swimming. But he was more worried about her. This had to have caught her flatfooted.

He'd pictured meeting the train and Jesse Rose stepping off, but he'd never really believed it was going to happen. And then for her to already know about not only Hank's death but her own kidnapping and illegal adoption… It blew his mind. At least Hank had taken care of that.

Why, though, had he kept it all from not only the rest of the world, including the McGraws, but he'd kept it from C.J.? Didn't he realize how much this was going to hurt her? Not to mention Jesse Rose knew all about C.J. but C.J. knew nothing about Jesse Rose all these years? Clearly Hank was involved in this. How much, though?

As he parked in front of the café, Boone said, "I thought we could have something warm to drink before we go out to the ranch."

Inside, they took at table at the back. Because of the hour, the café was empty. Fortunately, Abby, his brother Ledger's fiancée, wasn't working. The waitress who took their order said hello to Boone and merely smiled at the two women he was with.

"I feel as if I've always known you," Jesse Rose said to C.J. "I've heard so much about you from Uncle Hank for years. He said that he just knew the two of us would hit it off because we are so much alike. He promised that one day we would meet."

"I'm sorry to seem so surprised but Hank never told me anything about you," C.J. said.

Jesse Rose frowned. "I guess I understand under the circumstances. I always wondered why Uncle Hank wouldn't let me come out and visit. I thought it was just my mother's doing. She and Uncle Hank…

well, they didn't get along. But I adored him and he... I don't have to tell you how special he was." Tears filled her green eyes. "I'm so sorry he's gone."

"He had cancer," C.J. said as if seeing Boone's confusion. "He'd told her that he might not be able to meet the train. Apparently, he knew he didn't have long."

"Oh, wow, I'm so sorry," Boone said to C.J. Just another thing Hank had kept from her.

"You never suspected you were adopted until you found the letter?" C.J. asked.

Jesse Rose hesitated before she said, "Not really. Don't most kids think they must have been adopted if they aren't that much like their parents or siblings? I didn't have siblings." She shrugged.

"So you aren't like your parents?" Boone asked.

Jesse laughed. "My father was blond and blue-eyed and so is my mother. She always told me that my dark hair came from my father's side of the family." She sobered. "Do you think there is any chance that there's a mistake and I'm not Jesse Rose Mc-Graw?"

"We won't know for sure until we do a DNA test, if you're agreeable, but you look just like our mother when she was your age," Boone said.

Jesse Rose brightened. "How strange and yet wonderful to find out that I might have siblings. I used to dream of having a brother or sister. I was so anxious on the train. That was the longest twenty hours of my life, but I'm like Uncle Hank. I hate to fly. Not that there was any way to fly into Whitehorse except by private plane."

"I'm sure Hank told you, but it isn't just siblings you have, but a twin," Boone said.

She nodded excitedly. "I can't wait to meet him. It's so strange. I've always felt like I was missing a part of myself. I know that sounds crazy."

"Not at all. I've heard that about twins, even fraternal twins."

"Will he be at the ranch when we get there?" When Jesse Rose saw them exchange a look, she asked, "What?"

"No, but he lives around here. His name is Tough Crandall. He ranches in the next county. It's just that he's known he was Oakley McGraw for years but he wants nothing to do with the notoriety that might come from it," Boone said.

"The kidnapping case was fairly well-known," C.J. added. "I hope you aren't worried about that part." Boone couldn't bear for Travers not to at least get to meet his only daughter.

Jesse Rose shook her head. "But if I was kidnapped and my mother knew…" She looked up, those green eyes bright with worry. "My mother wouldn't go to jail, would she?"

"We would do everything possible to keep that

from happening. We don't know what your mother was told. Oakley's mother believed she was saving him. Your mother might have, as well."

"Still, I don't understand how my mother could take someone's child," Jesse Rose said.

Chapter Eighteen

All the way out to the ranch, C.J. could see that Jesse Rose was struggling with the news of her uncle's death. It was clear that they were very close even though they hardly saw each other.

She also seemed nervous, not that C.J. could blame her. She was about to meet a family she'd never known, come back to a home she'd only lived in for six months as a baby, face a father who had missed her for twenty-five years.

"Did Hank tell you how you happened to be adopted by your mother?" C.J. finally had to ask.

"No, but he said he would explain everything." Tears welled in her eyes again. "I still can't believe he's gone."

"There's something you should know," C.J. said. "Hank didn't die of cancer. He was killed in a hit-and-run accident," she said. "One of the kidnappers is still at large and we think he might have…" She reached for Jesse Rose's hand and squeezed it. "I didn't know about the cancer. He kept a lot from me."

"I'm so sorry he kept his family from you," Jesse Rose asked. "He *adored* you. He told us such wonderful stories about you. You were like a daughter to him."

Jesse Rose's words filled C.J.'s heart to near bursting. "How often did he visit you?"

"Just once or twice a year. He said he was too busy to come more than that. I always asked to come visit him but he made excuses. Mother said it was because of the way he lived, like a pauper."

"I'm afraid there might be more to the story," Boone said.

Jesse Rose chuckled. "That Hank was rich." She nodded at her brother's surprise. "His family was very wealthy, but he never wanted anything to do with the money. He wanted to find his own way in life without them telling him what to do. I guess my grandparents almost disowned him when he became a private investigator and moved to Butte, Montana."

"That explains a lot," Boone said and glanced in the rearview mirror back at C.J.

She smiled at him, also glad there was at least one thing she didn't have to worry about. The stocks and bonds Hank had left her hadn't been appropriated by ill-gotten means.

"This is beautiful," Jesse Rose said as she looked out at the country.

It was nothing like Butte, C.J. thought. Butte sat in a bowl surrounded by mountains. This part of Montana was rolling prairie. The only mountains she could see were the Little Rockies on the horizon. She thought about what Boone had said about the country growing on her. Maybe. Look how Boone McGraw had grown on her.

Boone drove up the lane to the ranch house, white wooden fences on each side of the narrow road. Yesterday C.J. had been driving and too anxious to pay much attention. Now she took it all in. The ranch reminded her of every horse movie she'd ever seen as a girl. Miles of pasture fenced in by white-painted wooden fence that made the place look as if it should be in Kentucky—not the backwoods of Montana.

In the front seat, Jesse Rose let out a pleased sound at the sight of a half dozen horses running beside the SUV on the other side of the fence, their tails waving in the wind.

"I love horses. It's one reason I've always wanted to come to Montana. But Uncle Hank…" Tears filled her eyes again. She wiped them. "I always knew he was hiding something from us, but I just assumed it was his lifestyle."

Boone pulled up in front of the large ranch house

and cut the engine. "Hope you're ready to meet the family, because they are more than ready to meet you."

The family had come spilling out the door, clearly unable to hold back. C.J. stood back to watch as Travers came down the steps. He took one look at Jesse Rose and pulled her into a hug. It was a beautiful sight, all of the McGraws and future McGraws welcoming Jesse Rose.

And Jesse Rose seemed smitten with all of them as they quickly ushered her inside.

"Hey," Boone said, suddenly next to her. "You all right?"

She wiped at her eyes and nodded, unable to speak.

"I'm sorry about Hank," he said as got Jesse Rose's suitcase from the back and they stepped out of the falling snow and onto the porch.

"Sounds like the killer did him a favor since everyone said he died instantly. I just wish…"

"I know." He put his arm around her and she leaned into his strong, hard body. He smelled good, felt good. She thought she could have stayed right there forever.

But from inside the house, his father called to him. "Champagne!"

JUST OUTSIDE OF WHITEHORSE, Cecil's cell phone rang, making him jump. He saw that it was Tilly. Now what?

"Hey," he said, trying to sound upbeat.

"You can't believe what is happening here," Tilly whispered.

His stomach roiled. Tilly sounded like she might bust if she didn't tell someone.

"Jesse Rose. She's been found. She came in on the train today and Boone and the female private investigator just brought her out to the ranch. Everyone is so excited."

Not everyone. "Must have been a shock to Jesse Rose."

"Didn't sound like it. Apparently she knew—that's why she came out on the train to meet her family. I have no idea how long she's known. Travers is beside himself." He heard her admiration for her boss in her voice and growled under his breath. "Where are you?"

"I'm headed back home," he said as he saw the outskirts of Whitehorse. But he needed time to think.

In fact, he'd asked her not to mention that they were back together. He knew what Travers McGraw thought of him. A lot of people thought he was a loser.

"There is going to be a huge celebration out here tonight," Tilly was saying. "The twins have been found. Bless the Lord."

Yes, he thought, his leg aching.

"When Boone called, did he say who the other kidnapper was?" He held his breath.

"I didn't get to hear all of the conversation," Tilly said, sounding so excited she was breathing hard. "But some letters came today from that private investigator I told you about. And a package from the second Mrs. McGraw."

He heard the distaste in his ex-wife's tone. "A package from Patty? You sure it's not a bomb?"

"Very funny. No, it feels like a book. It's addressed to Mr. McGraw."

A book? He brushed that away. It was the letters that he was worried about. "Who are the letters to?"

"There's one for Jesse Rose, one for that young female private eye, C.J. West, that Boone brought back with him and one for Mr. McGraw."

"Travers?" This was it. His worst fear was coming true. He looked at Whitehorse ahead. He could just keep driving to North Dakota and beyond, but they would eventually find him. Or maybe there was a chance… "So you haven't given anyone the letters yet?" he asked, praying she hadn't.

"No, everyone is too excited to see Jesse Rose," Tilly said.

"Don't give them the letters! Tilly, are you listening to me?"

"Yes, but why wouldn't I—"

"You can't give them the letters." He racked his brain as to what to do. "Burn them."

"I can't do that!"

"Then hold on to them until I get there. Can you do that?" His mind was whirling. If the McGraws knew the part he'd played in the kidnapping, then he would have heard by now. Tilly would have heard. So the little female PI hadn't found out anything.

Instead, Hank had written letters, letters that would incriminate them both. He swore under his breath. "Tilly, just do as I ask, please."

"I don't understand why you would want me to—"

"Tilly, if you love me, if you've ever loved me, I'm begging you, hide the letters. I'm on my way out there. I will explain everything when I get there."

"SOMETHING WRONG?" BOONE ASKED, making Tilly jump. She had her back to him as she was talking on the phone. She hadn't heard over the commotion in the other room.

He was still in shock. In his wildest dreams, he'd hoped Jesse Rose would get off that train. But he'd never imagined that she would already know about him and the rest of the McGraws—let alone know about C.J.

Uncle Hank? He'd seen C.J.'s expression. She'd been poleaxed by the news. What they didn't know was how Hank's sister had come to have Jesse Rose. Had Hank been involved in the kidnapping?

From everything he'd learned about the man after talking to people in Butte—including C.J.—he found it hard to believe. But the man had known that Jesse Rose had been kidnapped and he hadn't come forward. Until now, Boone thought. Hank had finally come forward after twenty-five years. Because he knew he was dying?

Travers had insisted they have champagne so he'd come into the kitchen hoping to find their new cook, but had found Tilly instead. When he'd heard the shrill rise of her voice on the phone, he'd been worried something might have happened.

But now she quickly stuffed whatever she'd been holding into her large purse along with her phone before she turned. She put on a big smile, making him all the more concerned that she was hiding something.

"If there is anything I can do…" he said seeing that she appeared to be trembling.

"Oh, you are so sweet. You're whole family. I… I feel so fortunate to work here. Your father…he's been so nice to me all these years, and letting me come back to work the way he did…" She sounded close to tears.

"Tilly," he said, stepping to her to take her shoulders in his hands. "You are family to us. That's why you can tell me if something is wrong."

She nodded, tears in her eyes. "It was Cecil on the phone…" She looked at the floor and, taking a deep breath, let it out before she continued. "He doesn't want anyone to know that we're thinking about getting back together."

Boone smiled. "Well, that's good news, isn't it?"

"Yes, of course. Cecil is just worried that people will talk or worse, you know."

He did know. He remembered years ago when Tilly and Cecil had gotten a divorce. Cecil had never been one to work and Tilly had put up with it for years and had finally had enough. Everyone had thought she should have kicked him out a lot sooner. Those same people would probably think she was a fool for taking him back.

"If you're happy, then I'm happy for you," he said. "I just wanted to check and see what room we might put Jesse Rose in."

"Oh, let me show her." Tilly started to head toward the living room, but quickly turned back to grab her purse. "I'll just put this away first."

"I'M SURE YOU all have a lot of questions," Jesse Rose said after glasses of champagne were raised to celebrate her return. "I have a lot myself. But I am so happy to learn about all of you. I always wanted siblings. I can't believe this." She smiled as she looked around the room, her gaze lighting on C.J. for a long moment. "I especially always wanted a sister."

C.J. smiled, happy for Jesse Rose, but feeling like she didn't belong here. Once it came out about Hank... Boone took her barely touched champagne glass and set it aside. His fingers brushed hers as he did, making her start. Their gazes locked for a moment.

"You okay?" he whispered.

She smiled and nodded, but she felt anything but okay and Boone seemed to sense it. He took her hand and led her down a hallway to a sunroom off the south side of the house. "You should be back there with your family," she protested when he let the door close behind them.

"I can see that you're not okay," he said, stepping to her to lift her chin with his warm fingers. "Tell me what's bothering you?"

"I shouldn't be here. This is family—"

"You're with me."

Her pulse leaped at the look in his eyes.

"I want you here. I... I want you."

Before she could move, he pulled her to him. The kiss on the train platform had stirred emotions and desires in her. But it was nothing like this kiss. C.J. couldn't remember ever feeling such swift, powerful emotions course through her. Desire was like a fire inside her that had been banked for too long. Boone deepened the kiss, sending her reeling with needs that she'd kept bottled up. She leaned into him, wanting...

There was a sound outside the door.

He pulled back, his gaze on hers, the promise in those blue eyes fanning the flames.

"Boone!" His brother Cull stuck his head in.

"Oh, there you are." Cull looked embarrassed. "Sorry. Dad needs you."

"Go," C.J. said as she tried to catch her breath. "I'm just going to step outside for a moment. It's hot in here."

Cull was grinning at his brother as they both left.

C.J. grabbed her coat and stepped outside, practically fanning herself with the freezing-cold evening air. Twilight had fallen over the ranch, gilding it and the fresh snow in a pale silver. Cooling down, she pulled on her coat as she looked to the Little Rockies. She thought about what Boone had said about this part of Montana growing on her. It had. Just as Boone McGraw had.

But it was his words just moments ago that still had the fires burning in her. *I want you here. I want you.* She'd heard how hard those words were for him to say.

Her heart was still pounding at the memory of the kiss, to say nothing of the promise she'd seen in his blue eyes, when she heard a noise behind her.

Chapter Nineteen

Before she could turn, C.J. was grabbed from behind. She felt the cold barrel end of a gun pressed to her temple.

"Listen to me," the man whispered against her ear. "Do what I say or you die and so does everyone else in that house. You understand?"

She nodded and he jerked her backward as he half dragged her to the closest barn. She noticed that he was limping badly. This was the man who'd broken into her house. The same one Boone had seen at Hank's funeral. The same one who'd killed Hank and tried to run her and Boone down in Butte?

Once inside the barn, he said, "Call your boyfriend."

"What?" She'd been thinking about her self-defense training. The problem was that the man was large and strong and he'd caught her off guard. And now there was a gun to her temple. Something in the man's tone also warned her that he was deadly serious—and nervous as hell. "I don't have a boy-friend."

"Boone McGraw. I saw the two of you. Call him. Then hand me the phone."

"No." She wasn't going to ask Boone to come out here to face a man with a gun because she'd fallen in love with him. She'd rather die than—

"Listen to me. If you do this, no one will get hurt. If I have to haul you inside the house with this gun to your head, a whole lot of people are going to die. My wife is inside that house and she has some letters I need. Once I have those, you can both go back to your lives. No one gets hurt. Otherwise…"

She thought of Boone's family. She couldn't chance that the man was telling the truth about more people being hurt. Also this would buy time and give her a chance to get out of this.

"You're the one who broke into my house," she said as she got a glimpse of the man with the scar on his face and the black baseball cap covering his graying hair. "You were at Hank's funeral."

He grunted. "Make the call." He held her tighter, the barrel of the gun pressing hard against her temple. She'd had self-defense training for her job. Hank had insisted. But he'd also warned her about acting rash.

Some of these people are all hopped up on God only knows what, he'd told her. *Best to bide your time, try to talk your way out of the situation and if all else fails, use your training.*

She doubted there would be any talking her way out of this. She could feel the man's nerves vibrating through his body. He was too jumpy. In the state he was in, he might pull the trigger accidentally. But that meant there was a good chance of him making a mistake and giving her an opening to escape. She had to count on that. If she got the chance, she would do what she had to do to keep him from killing both her and Boone.

"Okay." Pulling out her phone, she made the call with trembling fingers.

He snatched the phone away from her before she could say a word. "Boone? Just listen if you don't want your girlfriend to die. I have a gun to her head. I need you to find Tilly. She has some letters. Tell her to give them to you and then come outside. Once I see that you have the letters, I will let your girlfriend go."

BOONE LISTENED. SOMEONE had C.J.? Had a gun to her head over some…letters? He recalled earlier when he'd startled Tilly. She said she'd been on the phone with her ex-husband, but had said what he'd overheard had something to do with them getting back together.

He now realized it had been a lie. He excused

himself and went looking for Tilly. He thought about taking one of his father's guns, but he didn't want to call attention to himself by going into the gun room where all the guns and ammunition was locked up.

And if anyone in the family knew where he was going, they would want to come with him. He couldn't chance what the man might do. The man on the phone had sounded scared. And maybe unstable. Surely he didn't believe he was going to get away with this, whatever it was.

He found Tilly in one of the bedrooms. "Tilly?"

She'd been pacing and now jumped at the sound of her name. The woman was literally wringing her hands.

"You have some letters?" he said, not having time to find out what was wrong with her right now.

Her eyes widened. "You know about the letters?"

"I was told to get them from you."

She nodded, looking like she might burst into tears. "He told me to keep them. I—"

"It's fine. Just give them to me."

Tilly moved to a table next to the bed where she'd apparently come to clean, picked up her large bag and dug into it, pulling out one business-size envelope after another until there were three on the bed. She handed them to him.

"I just did what he asked me to do," she said.

Boone nodded as he took the letters, noting the

names on them and the return address. They were all from Hank Knight. "Who asked you to keep the letters a secret, Tilly?"

"Cecil." She looked confused. "My ex-husband. Isn't he the one who wants the letters?"

C.J. COULD FEEL the man getting more impatient by the moment. He kept looking toward the house and muttering under his breath as he held her tightly, the gun to her head.

"This is about some letters?" she asked.

"As if you don't know. Your PI friend sent them."

"Hank?"

"One to you, one to Jesse Rose, one to Travers McGraw."

"What's in them?" she asked. But she already knew. The answers they all desperately needed.

"Don't you wish you knew? Once they're destroyed, it will finally be over."

She doubted that, but she didn't think telling him would do either of them any good. "The kidnapping," she said with a sigh. "You're afraid there is something in them that incriminates you." She felt her pulse jump. "You think Hank knew who was behind the kidnapping. That's why you killed him." Anger filled her. "And you thought I might discover the truth. Why else would you try to run me down in

Butte? You were the kidnapper's accomplice. Now you have a gun to my head? Are you crazy?"

"Crazy like a fox. Without proof there is nothing anyone can do. I got away with it for twenty-five years. If you're partner hadn't stirred things back up…"

She could tell that the man was unhinged. Fear made her heart pound. And now Boone was on his way.

The back door of the house opened and Boone stepped out. He held up what looked like three business-size envelopes.

The man pushed C.J. out of the barn door far enough so Boone could see her. Even from the distance, she could see his jaw tighten as he saw the gun pointed at her head. He started toward them in long strides.

Since hearing of Hank's death, all she'd thought about was finding his killer. Now his killer was right here, but all she could think about was Boone. *I've fallen in love with this man. I can't let this man kill him.*

"Cecil Marks?" Boone called, stopping a few yards short of the barn door. "Let her go and you can have your letters."

"BRING THE LETTERS into the barn," Cecil called back.

Boone shook his head. "Not until you let her go."

"Bring in the letters or I'm going to shoot her and then you!" Cecil was losing it. C.J. could feel him coming apart, his body shaking as if all this had finally gotten to him. "I have nothing to lose at this point. I've already killed two people. You think I won't kill two more? Bring them now or so help me—"

Boone started toward the barn.

C.J. told herself that maybe the man would take the letters and run off. Maybe the best thing was to just hand them over—

"Cecil!"

They all looked toward the house as an older blonde woman came out into the snow. C.J. felt the barrel of the gun move a few inches against her head as Cecil saw her.

"Tilly? Go back. Everything is going to be all right. But you have to go back into the house." Cecil's voice broke.

"I can't let you do this!" Tilly cried and kept coming toward them.

"No, go back!" He was shaking hard now.

C.J. realized she was watching a man come apart at the seams. Boone must have seen it, too.

"Tilly, don't make me do this!" Cecil cried as he dragged C.J. back a step.

She knew there was no longer any time. If she didn't act now...

Preparing herself for the worst, she kicked back at the man's bad leg and let all her weight fall forward, becoming dead weight in the man's single arm holding her. At the same time, she saw Boone rush them.

Cecil let out a scream of pain and began to fall forward with her. He had to let go of her as she fell. She didn't feel the cold barrel of the gun against her temple anymore, she thought, an instant before she heard the deafening sound of the gun's report.

As she dropped to the ground, she saw Boone barrel into the man. The two went flying backward. From the ground, she saw Boone on top of Cecil struggling for the gun. The sound of the gun's first report still ringing in her ears, she started to get up when the gun went off again.

This time it was Tilly who screamed at the entrance to the barn. C.J. turned to see the woman's chest blossom red before she dropped to the ground.

Cecil let out a cry as he saw Tilly fall. Boone wrenched the gun from the man's hand and slammed him down hard to the barn floor. C.J. could hear voices and people running from the house.

The next moment, she was in Boone's arms. Her brothers had Cecil. She'd seen Nikki on the phone to the sheriff and a sobbing Cecil Marks was being restrained as he tried to get to his wife.

From the barn floor, Travers McGraw picked up the three letters Boone had dropped.

Chapter Twenty

"The sheriff just brought these by," Boone said when he found C.J. in the sunroom.

C.J. took the envelope from him and just held it for a long moment. She was still shaken by everything that had happened. Cecil was in jail. She'd heard that he'd completely broken down and confessed everything. Tilly was dead, having died on the way to the hospital.

A minute didn't go by that C.J. wasn't reminded how easily it could have been one of them in the morgue right now. That Boone could have been killed… It gave her waking nightmares.

"If you want to be alone when you open it…" Boone said.

"No." She met his gaze and smiled before patting the cushion on the couch next to her. "I suspect this is about the kidnapping. Has your father opened his letter yet? Or Jesse Rose?"

"They're reading theirs now," he said as he joined her.

Carefully she opened the flap and took out the letter.

Dear C.J.,

If you're reading this, I am no longer with you. I didn't want you to worry about me, that's why I didn't tell you. I'm sorry. I figured you would have enough to deal with once I was gone without knowing that I was dying. I had an amazing life. I don't regret any of it. But you, C.J., you were the light of my life. I can't imagine what it would have been like without you in it from the time you came charging into my office, looked around and said, "What a mess!" You were five.

She laughed as tears welled. Boone, who'd been reading along with her, handed her a tissue. She wiped her eyes and continued reading.

I hope that by the time you read this, you'll have met Jesse Rose. Isn't she wonderful? And that you will see that she makes it home to her birth family, the McGraws.

I've confessed my part in all this to Travers McGraw in the letter I wrote him. But I wanted you to know, as well. Years ago, Pearl Cavanaugh contacted me. She had a child that desperately needed a home. It wasn't the first time I'd helped with adoptions from the women of the Whitehorse Sewing Circle. I never asked where the babies came from. I just trusted that I was helping the infant—and the desperate family that wanted a child.

At the time my sister had been trying to have a baby and after numerous miscarriages had been told it would never happen. The moment I laid eyes on the little girl who was brought to me, I fell in love with Jesse Rose. I knew who she was. It was in all the news. But I also knew from Pearl that it was felt that the infant wasn't safe in the McGraw house.

I should have done the right thing. But at the time, the right thing felt like not returning her. When I handed Jesse Rose to my sister… Well, I've never felt such emotion. No little girl could have been more loved.

Maybe it was knowing I was dying. Or maybe it was seeing Travers McGraw on television pleading for information about his daughter. I called the lawyer to make sure the baby I'd given my sister really was Jesse Rose McGraw. Then I couldn't keep it from Jesse Rose and the McGraw family any longer. I flew to Seattle and told Jesse Rose and my sister what had to be done.

It was the hardest thing I'd ever done—short of keeping all this from you, C.J. Truthfully, I was a coward. I couldn't bear to see your expression when you heard what I'd done all those years ago. I hope you can forgive me.

I also hope you and Jesse Rose will meet. She's always wanted a sister and you two are the joys of my life.

I will miss you so much.

Hank

Tears were streaming down C.J.'s face as she finished the letter. Boone pulled her into his chest, rubbing her back as she cried.

"I know what he did was wrong, but I miss him," she said between sobs.

"I know."

When she finally pulled herself together, she straightened. "There was nothing in the letter about Cecil Marks. What if Hank knew nothing about his part in the kidnapping? What if—"

"If Cecil was free and clear and would never have been caught if he hadn't panicked?" Boone shook his head. "Apparently Tilly had told him that Hank had called our lawyer and knew something about

Jesse Rose and the kidnapping. Cecil had believed it was true."

"So if he hadn't confessed…"

"We would never have known the part he played in the kidnapping."

She nodded, shocked at the irony.

"Maybe there is something in my father's letter," Boone said. "But it doesn't sound like Hank knew who the kidnapper's accomplice inside the house was."

"I need to go find Jesse Rose," C.J. said, getting to her feet. "If her letter is anything like mine…"

BOONE THOUGHT OF his father. Anxious to find out what had been in his letter, he found Travers in his office. The letter he'd received was lying open on the desk. His father looked up as he came in.

"Are you all right?" Boone asked.

"Yes." The older man nodded. There were tears in his eyes. "It's good to know what happened. Jesse Rose was raised by loving parents. That's all that matters. And now she is home. She wants to stay out here on the ranch. She has a degree in business. I think she can be an asset to the ranch and take some of the load off my shoulders. What do you think?"

Boone chuckled. "I think you're an amazing man. You are so forgiving."

His father shrugged. "If I have learned anything

it's that holding a grudge is harder on you than on the person who wronged you. I don't have time for regrets. I just want to spend the rest of my life enjoying my family and it's almost Christmas. The doctors say that your mother can start coming home for visits after the first of year. If those go well... So tell me about C.J."

"What do you want to know?" Boone asked, startled by the change of topic.

"When you're going to ask her to marry you," his father said with a laugh as he leaned back in his chair.

"I barely know the woman."

"I guess you'd better take care of that, then."

C.J. FOUND JESSE ROSE in her room. The door was open so she tapped on it and stepped in to hand her a clean tissue. Jesse Rose laughed, seeing that C.J. was still sniffling, too. They hugged and sat down on the edge of the bed.

"Hank hoped we'd be friends," Jesse Rose said.

"How can we not be?" she said. "We're the only two people who really knew Hank. It's strange, though, the way he brought us together."

"Even stranger the way he brought you and Boone together," Jesse Rose said with a teasing smile.

"You can't think he had a hand in that."

The other woman shrugged and winked. "If Hank

could have, he would have. You two are perfect for each other."

"I wouldn't say that exactly." C.J. felt herself blushing. "He's stubborn and bossy and impossible. On top of that, he's a cowboy."

Jesse Rose laughed. "It is so obvious that the two of you are crazy about each other. And every woman wants a cowboy."

"Not every woman," C.J. said with a laugh. "Anyway, I live in Butte and he…he lives here," she said, taking in the ranch with a wave of her hand.

"You don't want to stay on this amazing ranch? I'm going to. I've already talked to Travers…to my dad about it," Jesse Rose said. "It's going to take a little getting used to, calling him Dad and having four grown brothers—one a twin I still have to meet. But I love it here. I know this sounds crazy, but I feel as if this is really where I've always belonged."

C.J. laughed. "It is."

"I know, but after growing up in Seattle…" She shook her head. "I feel like I've come home."

"How is your mom taking it?"

"She's just glad she isn't going to prison."

"You sound angry with her."

Jesse Rose nodded slowly. "I guess I am a little. But Hank knew, too, and I can't be angry with him. I'm just so glad he told me the truth. Maybe my mom will come around. Travers—Dad has asked her to come out for a visit. Maybe she will."

BOONE LOOKED UP to see Jesse Rose and C.J. come into the living room. He was so thankful that C.J. had agreed to at least stay through Christmas.

"We were just discussing everything that has happened," Boone said as the two joined the rest of the family. "Nikki is finishing up her book now that we all know what happened the night of the kidnapping."

C.J. sat down next to Boone. "I still can't believe Cecil Marks thought Hank knew about the part he'd played."

"Apparently Tilly had told him she'd overheard us talking and that Hank knew who the accomplice was," Travers said. "Unfortunately, she got it wrong. Otherwise, we would have never known it was our housekeeper's ex-husband who worked with Howard Cline to kidnap the twins. Finally Marianne will now be cleared of any wrongdoing."

"Tilly was always listening to what was going on with all of us," Cull said. "She really did get caught in the crossfire this time, though."

Nikki elbowed him. "That's awful."

"Well, you know what I mean. It cost her her life."

"At least Cecil confessed to everything," Nikki said. "Now I can finally finish my book."

"So Cecil was never considered a suspect?" C.J. asked.

"Surely he was questioned the night of the kidnapping," Boone said.

"He was—once he regained consciousness," Nikki said. "He was in a car wreck on the other side of the county and ended up in a coma in the hospital the night of the kidnapping."

"Didn't anyone think that was suspicious?" C.J. asked.

"That was the problem. No one knew exactly what time the twins had been taken," Nikki said. "As it turns out, the twins had been missing for almost an hour before Patty was awakened and went in to check on them. By then, Cecil had stopped at a bar or two and gotten into a wreck. That was a pretty good alibi. Nor was there anything incriminating in his car. No one even knew he'd been out to the ranch that night since apparently Tilly was too doped up to mention it at the time and didn't think it important later I guess."

"Tilly never suspected him?" Cull asked in disbelief.

Nikki shook her head. "She'd taken cold medicine

and then he'd given her even more. She was completely out of it."

"At least now we know who put the codeine cough syrup in the twins' room to make our mother look guilty," Ledger said.

"Seems like the perfect crime," Travers said. "But *someone* knew Cecil was in the house that night." Travers had been sitting quietly until then. Everyone turned to look at him. "When the letters came, there was also a package delivered. The sheriff found it in Tilly's purse where she'd apparently put it as Cecil had asked her."

"From Hank?" C.J. asked.

Travers shook his head. "From Patty. It's your mother's diary," he said to his sons. "Marianne saw Cecil coming out of the twins' room that night. That's why she went in. Unfortunately, she failed to tell anyone because of the altered state she was in from being poisoned with arsenic. When the twins were kidnapped, she apparently didn't recall seeing him. But she wrote it in her diary. Because of the poison in her system, it's possible she didn't remember."

"Patty returned the diary?" Boone asked sounding shocked. "Why would she do that?"

"There was only a short note inside. It said, 'Sorry, Patricia.' It seems she's had it this whole time, planning to use it against us."

"Except for that page she put under my door to make Marianne look guilty," Nikki said.

"Yes," Travers agreed.

"But wait," C.J. said. "Who was poisoning your mother?"

The family all looked at one another. It was finally Nikki who spoke. "We don't know. Probably Patty, but there are two other suspects—the former ranch manager, Blake Ryan, and our former family attorney, Jim Waters. Both were in love with Patty and would have done anything for her."

"Let's hope once Patty goes to trial that it all comes out," Cull said. "I suspect all three will be found guilty."

Travers got to his feet. "All I care about is that Cecil's confession clears your mother. Not that I ever believed she was in on the kidnapping. Even if Patty had been poisoning her and making her forgetful and confused, she wouldn't have hurt her babies."

"What will happen to Cecil?" Ledger asked.

"He'll probably get life. Kidnapping and deliberate homicide." Travers shook his head. "For twenty-five years he thought Harold Cline had double-crossed him, when all the time Harold was dead and buried. The man also must have lived being terrified that the truth would come out. So when Nikki began investigating the kidnapping for her book and we released more information…"

"Cecil killed Frieda to keep her from talking, although I doubt she knew anything about who had helped Harold," Nikki said. "Once Tilly told her ex about the call from Hank…"

"Speaking of the upcoming trial, Jim Waters called," Cull said. "He swears he's being framed for the poisonings. He was practically begging for you to help him, Dad."

Travers sighed. "Jim got himself into the mess he's in—he's going to have to get himself out. I would imagine the truth will come out one way or another. Blake Ryan hasn't gotten off free, either. He's being investigated for co-conspiracy with Patty and Jim Waters in the poisonings."

"If all three of them were in on it, one of them will turn on the others," Boone said.

"Jim and Blake both thought they would have Patty and the ranch once you were out of the way, Dad," Cull said.

"So who is the father of Patty's daughter Kitten?" Ledger asked.

"Patty told me it was just some one-night stand," Boone said. "If you can believe Patty." The former nanny, turned second McGraw wife, had always had trouble with the truth, he added.

"You do realize that Patty will probably get off with no more than a few years in prison for what she did to this family," Cull said.

"Probably," Travers agreed. "It's impossible to prove that she was behind the poisoning of your mother all those years ago. But I think a jury will have a hard time believing that she wasn't behind my arsenic poisoning in one way or another."

"Well, it's finally over," Ledger said.

"Except for Patty's tell-all book," Cull said.

"Haven't you heard? Because of the hype around Nikki's book about what really happened, the other publisher decided they weren't interested in Patty's," Travers said and smiled. "Explains why she returned the diary. But apparently she got to keep the advance to pay her lawyer."

A log popped in the fireplace and as darkness descended on the ranch, Boone put his arm around C.J. and looked at the Christmas tree, bright with lights and ornaments.

Ledger's fiancée, Abby, and Jesse Rose came in from the kitchen with plates of sandwiches. They were both laughing about something Jesse Rose had said.

"I don't think I ever believed in happy endings until this moment," Boone said and smiled at his father.

"All that matters is that the twins were found. They've both had good lives. That's all I could have hoped for," Travers said and smiled. "That's all I *did* hope for."

Epilogue

A year later, the family all gathered in the living room on Christmas Eve to celebrate. And they had a lot to celebrate, Travers McGraw thought as he looked at his burgeoning family.

He watched his oldest son, Cull, pour the champagne—and the nonalcoholic sparkling grape juice.

"So much has happened," Travers began, his voice breaking with emotion as he raised his glass in a toast. "I have my family back and so much more." He laughed and looked at the women who'd joined the family in the past year—all of them pregnant. "I never thought I'd live to see my first grandchild born, let alone four."

The room erupted in laughter. Cull and Nikki had started it by getting married and pregnant right after their wedding, then Ledger and Abby, then Boone and C.J.

"We have so much to be thankful for this holiday," he said and looked to his daughter, Jesse Rose. She'd moved in and was now working with the horse business right alongside her father. Travers had extended offers to her adoptive mother to come visit over the past year, but she hadn't come out to the ranch yet.

So much had happened but at least now the kidnapping was behind them. And Marianne would be coming home soon to stay. She'd come for a few visits, but the doctor said they needed to take it slowly. Finding out that she'd had nothing to do with the kidnapping had been huge in her recovery. That and seeing both of her once-lost babies now grown.

"You said Tough has been going by to see mother?" Cull asked.

Travers nodded and smiled. "He said it's gone well. She knew him right away."

"Unlike Vance Elliot," Cull said. "He fooled us for a while. I was starting to believe he really was our brother."

"Vance got his head turned by the idea of cashing in on becoming Oakley," Travers said. "He knew it was wrong."

"I heard that you paid for Vance's lawyer," Cull commented, clearly not approving.

"Yes, I did," his father said. "I saw something in him. In fact, when he gets out of jail, I've offered him a job."

"Dad, do you think that's a good idea?" Ledger asked.

"I do. He's had a rough life. I like to think that showing someone like him kindness can change him."

"Count the silverware," Cull said, but he patted his father's shoulder. "You always see the good in a person. I guess it's something to aspire to."

Boone laughed. "Nothing wrong with being a skeptic. It balances things out." C.J. poked him in the ribs.

Travers laughed. "I'd like to toast Nikki. If it hadn't been for her… Once she started asking questions, the truth started coming out. Thank you," he said, raising his glass. "And congratulations. I heard your book made the *New York Times* bestseller list the first week out."

They all raised their glasses.

"And to Jesse Rose," Travers said. "It is so wonderful to have you home."

BOONE LOOKED AT his beautiful wife. It was true what they said about being pregnant. C.J. glowed. He couldn't believe how quickly this past year had gone. Mostly he couldn't believe that not only had he gotten up the courage to ask C.J. to marry him, but that she'd accepted.

After Christmas last year, he'd driven her back to Butte. They'd talked a lot on the way home, but mostly about the kidnapping and Jesse Rose's return. C.J. had still been dealing with Hank's death and all the secrets he'd kept from her.

Back in Butte, he'd stayed to help C.J. clean out

Hank's office and close it for good. When he couldn't think of any other excuse not to return to the ranch, he'd finally realized that he couldn't live without this woman.

He'd asked her out to dinner, gotten down on one knee and proposed.

To his shock, she'd said yes.

He'd been even more shocked when she'd wanted to return to the ranch and give up her PI business in Butte.

It wouldn't be the same without Hank and I've fallen in love with your family, she'd said.

Just my family?

She'd laughed and thrown her arms around him. *I never thought I'd fall in love with a cowboy. But, Boone McGraw, you're the kind of cowboy who grows on a girl. Take me home, cowboy.*

THE LIGHTS ON the Christmas tree twinkled, the air rich with the smell of freshly baked gingerbread cookies and pine. C.J. breathed it all in, feeling as if she needed to pinch herself as she stood looking at this wonderful family scene. She wished Hank could see this. Maybe he could.

She felt Boone come up behind her. He encircled her with his arms. She leaned back against him and closed her eyes as his hands dropped to her swollen stomach, making her smile.

"Happy?" he whispered.

"Very." She opened her eyes and turned in his arms. "I've never had a family like this before."

"Well, you do now. I think Hank would be happy for you."

She nodded. "I was just thinking of him. It's all he ever wanted for me." But it was more than she had ever dreamed possible. When Boone had gotten down on one knee and asked her to marry him it had been the happiest day of her life.

C.J. had thought she couldn't give up her private investigator business. The truth was she wanted a family of her own far more. And now they were expecting. She couldn't wait.

What made it even more fun was that her two sisters-in-law were also expecting and Abby was pregnant with twin girls while she and Nikki were having boys. With all three families building on the ranch and not that far apart, their kids would all grow up together here.

She couldn't imagine anything more wonderful. Jesse Rose was as excited as anyone. All this family and soon all these babies.

Don't worry about me, Jesse Rose had said. *One of these days I'll find me a cowboy and settle down myself. But I'm never leaving Montana.*

"I feel like all of this is a dream," C.J. said now to her husband. "If it is, don't wake me up."

Boone laughed. "Merry Christmas, sweetheart, and many more to come," he said and leaned down to kiss her as the doorbell rang.

"Enough of that!" Cull called from where he and Nikki had gone into the kitchen to check on dinner. "Someone answer the door!"

"I've got it!" Boone gave her another quick kiss before heading to the door.

To BOONE'S SURPRISE Tough Crandall was standing on the doorstep.

"I was invited," Tough said, taking off his Stetson.

Boone studied his brother. There was no doubt that this cowboy was Oakley McGraw. But he was determined not to be one of them. *Good luck with that*, Boone thought.

"Of course you were invited," he said to his brother. "It's Christmas and like it or not, we're family." Tough didn't have any other family since both his adoptive parents had passed away. Nor did the stubborn cowboy want to be a McGraw, he'd said. But Travers had been visiting him on and off and had obviously somehow talked him into spending Christmas with them.

"Help me with the presents I have out in my truck?"

Boone laughed. "You got it." Together they went out and brought in all the gifts. "Hey, everyone,

Tough's here," Boone announced as they came back inside.

His brother actually smiled as he wiped his feet and stepped in.

Say what you will about the McGraws, they were the kind of family that grew on you—whether you liked it or not.

Travers smiled and held out his hand to Tough. "Glad you could make it, son. I don't believe you've met everyone," he said after a moment. He began to introduce each of the family and new additions as he went around the room.

When he got to Jesse Rose, he hesitated. Tough was looking at his twin sister wide-eyed. For the past year, Jesse Rose had been dying to meet her twin, but Tough had been dragging his feet.

"This is…Jesse Rose," their father said.

Tough shook her hand. Their eyes locked and the cowboy seemed to be at a loss for words. "I had no idea," he said, his voice breaking.

She laughed, smiling as she asked, "No idea what?"

"That I would feel…such a connection."

"We're *twins*. Plus we share quite a history, wouldn't you say?"

He nodded. "It's the first time I've really felt like I was a part of this family."

"Well, now that you have," Travers said, "you're

just in time for dinner. After that we're going to be opening presents."

"And singing Christmas carols," Jesse Rose said. "It's going to be our new tradition."

"I can see where we're going to have a lot more new traditions," Travers said, putting his arm around Tough and Jesse. "But you might change your mind about the carols when you hear my sons sing."

"Not all of them are tone-deaf," Tough said and grinned.

Boone listened to the good-natured ribbing during dinner. Later Jesse Rose brought out her guitar and began to play "Silent Night." C.J. came to stand by him. He pulled her close, his eyes misting over as he counted his blessings and his family began to sing.

* * * * *

Don't miss the first two books in the
WHITEHORSE, MONTANA:
THE MCGRAW KIDNAPPING *series:*

DARK HORSE
DEAD RINGER

Available now from Harlequin Intrigue!

Get 2 Free Books,
Plus 2 Free Gifts—
just for trying the Reader Service!

HARLEQUIN

INTRIGUE

YES! Please send me 2 FREE Harlequin® Intrigue novels and my 2 FREE gifts (gifts are worth about $10 retail). After receiving them, if I don't wish to receive any more books, I can return the shipping statement marked "cancel." If I don't cancel, I will receive 6 brand-new novels every month and be billed just $4.99 each for the regular-print edition or $5.74 each for the larger-print edition in the U.S., or $5.74 each for the regular-print edition or $6.49 each for the larger-print edition in Canada. That's a savings of at least 12% off the cover price! It's quite a bargain! Shipping and handling is just 50¢ per book in the U.S. and 75¢ per book in Canada.* I understand that accepting the 2 free books and gifts places me under no obligation to buy anything. I can always return a shipment and cancel at any time. The free books and gifts are mine to keep no matter what I decide.

Please check one: ☐ Harlequin® Intrigue Regular-Print   ☐ Harlequin® Intrigue Larger-Print
                              (182/382 HDN GLWJ)   (199/399 HDN GLWJ)

Name _____ (PLEASE PRINT)

Address _____ Apt. #

City _____ State/Prov. _____ Zip/Postal Code

Signature (if under 18, a parent or guardian must sign)

Mail to the **Reader Service:**
IN U.S.A.: P.O. Box 1341, Buffalo, NY 14240-8531
IN CANADA: P.O. Box 603, Fort Erie, Ontario L2A 5X3

Want to try two free books from another line?
Call 1-800-873-8635 or visit www.ReaderService.com.

*Terms and prices subject to change without notice. Prices do not include applicable taxes. Sales tax applicable in N.Y. Canadian residents will be charged applicable taxes. Offer not valid in Quebec. This offer is limited to one order per household. Books received may not be as shown. Not valid for current subscribers to Harlequin Intrigue books. All orders subject to approval. Credit or debit balances in a customer's account(s) may be offset by any other outstanding balance owed by or to the customer. Please allow 4 to 6 weeks for delivery. Offer available while quantities last.

HI17R

Vickie reached out and set her hand over Monica's. "I'm so
sorry."

Monica Verne looked at Vickie and nodded. Griffin thought
that Vickie's ability to feel with others and offer them real
comfort was going to be one of her greatest assets in joining
the Krewe. It was also going to be one of the most difficult
parts of the job for her to learn to manage. He lowered his
head for a moment; it was an odd time to smile. And an odd
time to think just how lucky he was. Vickie was beautiful
to look at—five foot eight, with long raven black waves of
hair and blue-green eyes that could change and shimmer like
emeralds.

She was also so caring—honest and filled with integrity.

He truly loved her. Watching her empathy and gentle touch
with Monica, he knew all the more reason why.

"My husband didn't kill himself!" Monica whispered
fervently.

"I don't think it's been suggested that he killed himself.

I believe they're considering it an accidental death," Griffin began.

"Accidental death, my ass! If there's any last thing I can do for Franklin, it's going to be to make someone prove that this was no accidental death!" Monica lashed out, indignant. She wasn't angry with Vickie—who was still holding her hand. Her passion was against the very suggestion that her husband's death had been through a simple slip—some misfortune.

She wagged a finger at Griffin. "You listen to me, and listen well. We were the best, Frankie and me. I swear it. When all else fell to hell and ruin, we still had one another… Franklin did not meet up with a friend! He did not break into that cellar to drink himself to death! I'm telling you, I knew my husband, he…"

She broke off, gritting her teeth. She was trying not to cry. The woman was truly in anguish; she was also furious.

"I don't know when he went out. I don't know why he went out—or how he wound up at the restaurant. I do know one thing."

"What is that, Mrs. Verne?" Vickie asked.

Monica Verne startled them both, slamming a fist on the coffee table. "My husband was murdered!"

The motion seemed to be a cue.

In the yard, a dozen birds took flight, shrieking and cawing.

Griffin could see them as they let out their cries, sweeping into the sky.

A murder of crows…

And an unkindness of ravens…

As poetically cruel as the death of Franklin Verne.

WICKED DEEDS
by New York Times *bestselling author Heather Graham.*
Available now from MIRA® Books.

www.Harlequin.com

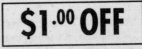

$1.⁰⁰ OFF

New York Times bestselling author

HEATHER GRAHAM

returns with the next
action-packed romantic suspense story
in the *Krewe of Hunters* series.

WICKED DEEDS

Available now.

mira
Harlequin.com

$8.99 U.S./$10.99 CAN.

$1.⁰⁰ OFF the purchase price of WICKED DEEDS by Heather Graham.

Offer valid from September 19, 2017, to October 31, 2017.
Redeemable at participating retail outlets, in-store only. Not redeemable at
Barnes & Noble. Limit one coupon per purchase. Valid in the U.S.A. and Canada only.

52615115

5 65373 00076 2 (8100)0 12306

® and ™ are trademarks owned and used by the trademark owner and/or its licensee.

© 2017 Harlequin Enterprises Limited

MCOUPHG1017